RENDEZVOUS WITH ROMANCE... AND DANGER

David slipped his arm around me while we stood outside the circle of lanterns that illuminated the driveway. The evening was warm and sweet-scented with late summer roses. I thought during those delicious moments that I wouldn't have minded standing there forever...

And then I saw him—the heavyset blond man from the bus depot at Harper's Fork. He stood across the driveway from us, close to one of the lanterns. The light shone directly on his mean, pouchy face as he watched the dancers closely. And I knew without a doubt that he was looking for me...

Other Avon Flare Books by
Jean Thesman

WHO SAID LIFE IS FAIR?

RUNNING SCARED

JEAN THESMAN

AN AVON FLARE BOOK

RUNNING SCARED is an original publication of Avon Books. This work has never before appeared in book form.

AVON BOOKS
A division of
The Hearst Corporation
105 Madison Avenue
New York, New York 10016

Published by arrangement with the author
Library of Congress Catalog Card Number: 87-91156
ISBN: 0-380-75230-1
RL: 4.7

First Flare Printing: August 1987

FLARE TRADEMARK REG. U.S. PAT. OFF. AND IN OTHER COUNTRIES, MARCA REGISTRADA, HECHO EN U.S.A.

Printed in the U.S.A.

K-R 10 9 8 7 6 5 4 3 2 1

To Rob and Dana

Chapter One

THE END OF SUMMER—warm, clear days scented with peaches ripening on the tree next to the porch and not a whisper of wind to disturb the leaves. I sighed, half asleep and contented with the whole world.

"Caroline," my mother called, startling me silly, "You're going to be staying with Grandma for a few days, and your cousin Jasper is going with you."

I sat straight up on the porch swing where I'd been daydreaming most of that hot August afternoon. "You're kidding!" I cried when I'd recovered enough to talk. "I'd love to visit Grandma, but I won't take Jasper—not even if you tie him up and gag him. What are you talking about, anyway?"

My mother had obviously planned a hit-and-run conversation because her feet were half-way through the door but the rest of her was leaning back toward the kitchen. "You know that Aunt Sybil and Uncle Ray are going to

Los Angeles," she said, smiling the way mothers do when they're up to something. How could I believe that smile when her eyes were absolutely furtive? "Well, your father and I decided to fly there with them. We'll be gone four days and you'll have a wonderful time with Gram. You always do."

All of her had oozed back in the house by the time she finished talking, but if she hoped that she had had the last word, she was wrong.

"I won't go with Jasper!" I shouted. "I refuse! I absolutely refuse! I'd rather die!"

Silence. Mother didn't even sneak a quick peek to see if I was standing at the top of the steps with a rope around my neck.

"I can stay here!" I shouted desperately, leaping out of the porch swing and running after her into the kitchen. "Jasper can go by himself. I'll visit Gram some other time."

"You can't stay alone in the house," Mom began as she put the kettle on the stove. She must have felt awfully guilty if she needed a cup of tea.

"I'm fifteen!" I protested. "I'm old enough to stay by myself."

"But Jasper shouldn't be on the bus without someone watching him." She avoided my eyes as she got a cup and a tea bag. "You know how he is."

Did I ever. My cousin Jasper was ten, which was bad enough. He was also a walking time bomb. Jasper *did* things. Or maybe I mean Jasper did *things*. Gram loved him, but everyone else developed a nervous twitch in his company. Even his parents.

"You bet I know how he is," I said, taking

out a cup for myself. "Which is why I'm not going. School starts next week, and I have no intention of spending four long, horrible days with a kid who collects garbage and thinks he's a bug."

Mother examined a fingernail as if she'd never seen it before. "Your father needs a rest. You know how hard he works. You wouldn't want to spoil everything, Caroline." She looked at me then, with big blue eyes just like mine. If I weren't also an expert at that helpless, innocent expression, I'd have been devastated.

I sighed, so she changed tactics. "I'll make you a deal," she wheedled. "If you go without a fuss, I think I can see my way clear to giving you a bonus. Look at it as a paid baby-sitting job. Once you're at Granite Ridge, Jasper will find plenty to do by himself. And Dad will drive up for you as soon as we get back, so you'll only have to be alone with Jasper tomorrow afternoon, on the bus."

"How big is the bonus?" I asked suspiciously. It would take a bundle to sweeten that four-hour bus ride. I love my mom, but she was asking me for a sacrifice beyond the call of family duty. Jasper's own mother had been known to clutch her head and mutter "Why me?" when his exploits were pointed out to her by raving teachers and furious neighbors.

Mom named a sum—about twice what I'd expected. Jasper must have developed some new and even more horrid habits, I thought as I nodded.

"I hope you know you're ruining my life," I told her, just to make sure she knew that money can't buy everything. I was sacrificing the last days of summer vacation.

"I'll bring you something nice from Los Angeles," she said as she poured boiling water into our cups.

"You'll have to bury it with me," I told her while I picked through a box of cookies, looking for my favorites. "Four hours on a bus with Jasper will probably kill me."

I took my tea and cookies out to the porch and sat on the swing, brooding. Visiting Gram in Granite Ridge is a a lot of fun. A month earlier, when I stayed there for a week, she taught me to play poker and drive her old truck. She's not like other grandmothers.

But then, Jasper wasn't like other cousins. He wasn't like anybody.

Four hours on a bus and four days in Granite Ridge with Jasper. The bonus didn't look so big after I'd had a chance to think about it.

The next morning I carefully packed everything I'd need into a big tote bag, and I was ready to leave when Aunt Sybil and Uncle Ray stopped by the house for me. At the last minute Mom and Dad decided to ride with us to the bus depot in Seattle. Maybe they thought it might take four adults instead of just two to load Jasper on the bus and keep me from running away. We all squeezed in Uncle Ray's station wagon, and I got stuck sitting next to Jasper.

"Hello, Miss Caroline Cartright," he said. Smart aleck. He'd broken his glasses again, I saw, and the frames were mended with tape. And his new jeans already had a rip in one knee. He has light brown hair like mine, but that day it was hanging over his eyes so that he looked like a dog peering out from under a ragged bedspread.

"Hello, Mr. Jasper Cartright," I replied as I wedged my tote between my feet. Then, to cut off any further attempts on his part to talk to me, I popped my headphones over my ears and turned my little radio on loud.

Jasper lifted one of the earpieces. "You want some gum?" he asked, holding out a lump of vile green bubble gum. It looked used.

"Barf," I responded and clapped the earpiece back in place.

My mother lifted the earpiece off my other ear. "Be nice," she hissed.

Stereo relatives. I smiled obediently at Jasper but still refused the gum. Something was stuck to it—lint, probably. I was afraid to ask. Jasper shoved the gum in his mouth and smiled back at me. His feelings never got hurt.

At the bus depot my dad, both mothers, Jasper, and I went inside while Uncle Ray parked the car. In one hand, Jasper carried a duffel bag with one pajama leg hanging out of it and in the other a huge stack of comic books lashed together with twine. The stack must have weighed half as much as he did. He owned a copy of every issue of "Bugman Adventures" ever printed and he never went anywhere without them. He quoted Bugman. Once he even tried to tattoo a picture of Bugman on the back of his hand, but his mother caught him in time. I had seen "Bugman Was Here!" spray-painted on walls all over Seattle, Washington, and I was certain Jasper was responsible.

"Bugman was in a bus depot once..." Jasper began.

"Hush," his mother said. "Tell Caroline on the bus." Oh, thanks a heap, I thought crossly.

She kept a firm grip on his arm—Jasper had a tendency to wander. "Now you're going to mind Caroline and behave yourself at Grandma's. Don't do what you did last time."

"What did he do?" I asked quickly.

"Never mind," both mothers said in unison.

My dad trotted up with the tickets just as Uncle Ray rushed through the door, and then it was time to leave. The bus departure was announced over the loudspeakers, parents kissed kids, and Uncle Ray slipped me a folded five-dollar bill while he hugged me. "Combat pay," he whispered.

Jasper dragged his duffel bag and precious collection of Bugman first editions up the bus steps while I lingered for one last opportunity to inflict agonizing guilt on my parents.

"I really have to do this?" I pleaded.

"It will strengthen your character," Dad said.

"But it never strengthened mine," Aunt Sybil said bewilderedly to Dad as I climbed the steps.

Jasper leaped into a seat halfway back in the nearly empty bus. Not many people go from Seattle to Granite Ridge, but the bus would pick up more passengers along the way. It's an interesting trip if you're a people-watcher.

Jasper stowed his literary masterpieces

under the seat, then looked around to check out the possibilities for making a pest of himself. Immediately he saw someone he knew.

"Hey, Cissy!" he yelled, deafening everyone on the bus.

I saw a girl wearing a red vest just like the one I had on. She had blondish hair, too. On her lap, she carried a package about the size of a shoebox, gift-wrapped and tied with ribbon like a birthday present. When Jasper bellowed at her again, she waved and smiled weakly. But I didn't think that the unenthusiastic smile had as much to do with Jasper as it did with the bruise on the side of her face. She saw me staring and looked away. I realized how rude I was, gawking like that, but I was afraid that apologizing would only make things worse.

When I sat down next to Jasper, I noticed that his face was red.

"That's Cissy Merchant," he said. "She's really nice."

"Isn't she a little old for you?" I teased.

He fingered his glasses uncomfortably. "She's *really* nice," he said.

"I believe you," I told him.

"Except that I wish she hadn't gone and got married."

"Married!" I gasped. "She's just a teenager."

"She's twenty-two," he retorted. "She used to work at the grocery store in Granite Ridge. Don't you remember her?"

I didn't. Keeping up on the folks at Granite Ridge never had very high priority with me when I visited Gram. I looked out the bus window and saw our parents waving. One more passenger boarded, the bus door closed, and we moved slowly away. I waved until my folks were out of sight.

The last passenger sat down in front of us and Jasper flopped over the back of that seat like a rag doll. "David!" he yelled. "Hey, David!"

"Sit down." I tugged at Jasper but it didn't help.

The passenger turned around and I took a good look. A very good look. Jasper's friend, this David, was a boy a little older than I was.

"What are you doing here?" he asked Jasper.

"I'm visiting Gram again," Jasper explained. "Me and my cousin Caroline."

The boy studied me with clear green eyes and then he smiled. "Caroline? Are you another Cartright?"

I nodded.

"I'm David Prescott. Jasper and I are old pals." He brushed dark hair away from his forehead. "How long are you staying in Granite Ridge?"

"Four days," Jasper answered for me. "David, can I ride your horse?"

"If your grandmother says so." David smiled at me again, dazzling me completely. In all the times I'd stayed with Gram, I'd never met him. I would have remembered—David was absolutely gorgeous. When he turned away, I was disappointed.

Jasper leaned back in his seat. "David has a horse," he said unnecessarily. "Sometimes he lets me ride her. I bet he'd let you ride her, too."

"We'll see." I didn't know anything about horses, but I was willing to learn.

Jasper pulled his stack of Bugman comics out from under his seat, untied it, selected one, and tied the stack up again. Hoping that he would occupy himself for the whole trip with this tasteful material, I took a book out of my tote and settled down to read, too.

Five seconds later, Jasper said, "You know Cissy?"

"I already told you that I didn't," I said, turning a page.

"She sure is nice."

"You told me a hundred times already."

"But she really is."

"I know."

"No, you don't know," Jasper said, agitated. He peered at me through his dirty glasses. "She's like Princess Sting in my Bugman comics. See?" He thrust a comic book in my face, with one grubby finger pointed at a voluptuous cartoon female done up in a hornet costume. A hornet with a thirty-eight-inch bust. Good grief.

"I'm sure Cissy is just like her," I said, pushing away the comic book. It's going to be a long, long ride, I thought.

"You don't say it like you mean it," Jasper complained.

"I mean it," I said, wondering if David could hear this inspiring conversation.

"She saved my life."

Now he had my full attention. I stared at him. "Sure she did. Listen, Jasper, you've got to quit pretending that Bugman is real. You're too old for that stuff. He's just a comic book character. Princess Sting is only a—"

"She did! Cissy, I mean. She saved my life, only I'm not supposed to talk about it. Gram says it gives people the wrong idea about what I do when I'm in Granite Ridge."

"What are you talking about?" I whispered, alarmed now.

Jasper fidgeted. "I can't tell. But it's true."

I leaned close to him. "You tell me and do it right now! I want to know ahead of time what sort of messes you get into when you're at Gram's."

I had to wait while Jasper pulled out his collection, returned his priceless volume to its place, retied the stack, and shoved it back again.

"It was when I went up the ridge to Piper's Rock," he said.

"What is Piper's Rock?" I asked, mystified. I had never heard of it.

"It's a place where nobody goes anymore. Not since the men with guns moved into the old farm."

"What old farm? What men?" I whispered, gritting my teeth. This was going to take all day.

"The men with guns. And Cissy married one of them."

Chapter Two

JASPER'S STORY SCARED ME. He'd gone exploring in the woods behind Gram's place, climbed the ridge, and when he got to the top—where this Piper's Rock is located—he saw that an old farm on the other side wasn't deserted anymore.

Instead of minding his own business, he walked to the farm. "Just to check it out," he said. "Like Bugman does."

Apparently Gram had told him to stay off the ridge because the people in town had been hearing gunfire there on and off all summer. (She hadn't told me to stay off the ridge when I was visiting her because I never go near it.) But Jasper never listened to anyone, not even Gram, and he was crazy about woods and other wild places. As I listened to him, I wondered why Gram let him out without a ball and chain fastened to his leg.

He knew he was doing something wrong—he admitted it—but he went right ahead and sneaked down the other side of the ridge to the farm. And he got caught.

"This guy grabbed me," he said, and his face turned so pale that his freckles stood out clear enough to count. "And he was yelling and dragging me away, but Cissy came then and told him to let go. She took me home and made me promise never to go back. I bet that man was going to kill me."

"He was only going to take you to the farm and call Gram to come and get you," I said, hoping I was right. "Don't make it sound worse than it is."

Jasper bit his lip. "That's what Gram says." He poked his glasses back up his nose. "You won't tell that I told you, will you? She can yell louder than anybody."

"She won't care," I assured him. "Maybe she'll tell me herself so I don't make the same mistake."

"That's true," he said, relieved. "Yes, that's what she'll do." He leaned back and sighed. "Cissy is really nice."

I looked around to see if the passengers in our part of the bus were listening. Most of the people were reading or looking out the windows—no one was paying attention to us. Good, I thought. Jasper's adventure embarrassed me. Leave it to him to trespass and get in trouble with a cranky farmer.

David Prescott seemed to be sleeping. The drone of the bus tires on the road was soothing, so I leaned my head back and dozed as we barreled north along the freeway.

"Caroline," Jasper whispered, shaking my arm. "Cissy's crying."

I opened my eyes, groaned, and looked around. Alone in the back of the bus, Cissy cried into a handful of tissues. The bruise on her face looked awful.

"She'll be fine," I told Jasper. "Don't worry." But neither of us believed that. Cissy didn't look at all fine.

"Maybe she was supposed to go to a birthday party in Seattle but when she got there, it was the wrong day," Jasper suggested hopefully.

I remembered the present she carried. "Maybe," I said. "Now close your eyes and sleep for a while."

"No, I think I'll count my cocoons," he said, and he fished a small paper sack out of the pocket of his jeans, opened it, and poured several dirty-looking cocoons into his palm. "Moths," he announced proudly. "Aren't they great?"

"Ugh."

"Would you rather see my old lottery tickets?" he asked earnestly as he dumped the cocoons back in the sack. "I've got 'em in my back pocket. I find 'em in gutters and trash cans, and I ask people to give them to me after they scratch the stuff off and find out they didn't win."

"Show me later. I'm sleepy," I told him. Losing lottery tickets and undeveloped bugs. What else? I put my headphones on again and tried to concentrate on a news broadcast, but frankly I couldn't have cared less about yesterday's big bank robbery, today's muggings, or tomorrow's heat wave. I had Jasper.

I awoke with a start. Jasper was shaking my arm and pulling on my headphones. "We're in Harper's Fork," he said, "And I have to go to the bathroom."

I must have slept a long time, because Harper's Fork is the last stop before Granite Ridge. Several people were getting off the bus, including Jasper's beloved Cissy. David's seat was empty, and I saw him outside the bus, heading toward the dingy little depot.

"I gotta go!" Jasper cried. If any of the people left on the bus had been in doubt about why Jasper wanted off, they weren't any longer.

"All right," I grumbled. "But that's all you're going to do." I followed him off the bus and into the depot. Just as I suspected, he passed right by the men's rest room and headed for a dreary little magazine stand tucked in one corner of the depot.

"Where are you going?" I grabbed for his arm and missed.

"First I want to see if the new Bugman comic is in."

I sighed and followed. I could see David feeding coins into a vending machine near the magazines. Two of us should be able to keep track of Jasper, I thought.

I saw Cissy, too, standing by a rack of paperback books, reading the titles as if they were desperately important to her. I walked over to her, not really sure why, but vaguely thinking that maybe someone ought to say something to her. She looked terrible.

"Hi," I said to Cissy, and she spun around nervously. "I'm Jasper's cousin Caroline, from Seattle."

She stuffed her tissues in one of the pockets in her red vest, but it was obvious she'd been crying—her eyes were bloodshot.

She cleared her throat, then said, "Hi." She was clutching the gift against her chest as if she thought I might grab for it.

"Are you going to a party?" I asked, to make conversation.

She backed away. "What?" she said. "What do you mean?"

"The present," I explained, pointing to it. "I wondered if you were going to a party."

She shook her head, then nodded. "It's a surprise," she said feebly.

I nodded and smiled. Weird. Obviously I was making her uncomfortable.

"See you later," I said finally, and I turned around and walked away as a metallic voice announced on the loudspeaker that a bus was leaving for Seattle. I should have left Cissy alone the way David did. He obviously knew her because he kept glancing at her, but he had enough sense to let her have her privacy.

He was drinking pop and standing guard while Jasper looked through the magazines, and I joined them, digging through the pockets in my vest, searching for change. If my cousin succeeded in locating the find of the century, another "Bugman Adventures," I'd probably have to pay for it. And time was running out, too.

"We have to get back on the bus," I told Jasper. "Did you find what you're looking for?"

"The new Bugman probably isn't out yet," David told me. I searched his face to see if he was hiding a grin. He wasn't.

"Don't tell me you like that awful stuff, too," I said.

"It grows on you. Jasper introduced me to Bugman and now I'm an addict." He looked up at the clock on the wall. "We'd better get going, Jazz."

"I haven't been to the bathroom yet," Jasper said.

"Hurry up!" I told him.

David winked one green eye at me. "I'd better supervise this mission."

"Thanks," I said, and I watched gratefully while David steered Jasper in the right direction, diverting him from searching through an ashtray for who-knows-what treasure and pulling him expertly away from a close examination of an old man sleeping on one of the benches.

The loudspeaker hissed and squealed and finally blatted out the information that the Seattle bus was pulling out and the Granite Ridge bus was leaving in five minutes. Several people headed for the door, and I hoped that David had heard the announcement. I'd hate to miss a bus and be stuck in a place like Harper's Fork with Jasper. I started toward the door, passed the paperback rack where I'd seen Cissy, and stopped dead.

She was gone but she'd left her package on top of the rack. I couldn't see her anywhere inside the depot, but, thinking that she might have gone into the rest room, I grabbed the present and ran toward the door marked

"Women." The room was empty but I yelled her name out anyway.

Maybe she'd gone out to the bus. I rushed through the door—and someone grabbed my arm, yanking me to one side.

"Let go!" I pulled loose and stepped back. A heavyset blond man wearing jeans and a plaid shirt was grinning down at me.

"Isn't that package for me?" he asked, reaching out one fat, dirty hand toward the gift I carried.

"No!" I said indignantly. "This belongs to Cissy Merchant."

The man scowled and hesitated for a moment. But suddenly he grabbed for the package. "Let me have it."

Scared silly, I held the package behind my back. "Get away from me!" But when I tried to edge past him, he blocked my way.

"No games, sweetheart. Hand it over."

My mouth went dry. He was serious. I wanted to give the package to him—after all, it was only a dumb birthday present—but I was too scared to move.

He stepped closer, still grinning. "Don't make trouble. I could hurt a pretty girl like you real bad."

A big man in a brown uniform hurried up and slipped between me and the man in the plaid shirt. "What's the problem here?" he boomed. The uniform was like the one our bus driver wore, but I couldn't have been more grateful if he'd been a police officer.

"This man..." I began, full of courage now that I had a protector.

"I made a mistake," the blond man said. "I

thought she was someone else." He backed up as he spoke, and then he turned and walked quickly out the door. He was glaring at me as he got into his gray truck.

"You okay?" the driver asked.

"Yes, yes," I babbled. I saw David hauling Jasper out of the men's room and herding him toward the door, so I yelled "Thanks!" and ran after them, scared we'd miss the bus.

I was the last one to board, and as I got on, I looked around to see if the blond man was watching me. I couldn't see him, but I was glad when the bus door shut behind me. Then I realized that I still had Cissy's package. And she wasn't on the bus. Oh well, I thought, I'll give it to her when we reach Granite Ridge.

David was in his seat, smiling as I came down the aisle. Jasper knelt in my place, but he scooted over next to the window to make room for me. The bus moved smoothly out to the street. I looked back and saw the gray truck had gone.

"You've got Cissy's present!" Jasper squalled as I sat down. "What are you doing with it?" He looked around, saw that she wasn't on the bus, and opened his mouth to yell again, but I pinched him.

"For heaven's sake, sit down and shut up," I said.

"Why do you have Cissy's present?" he demanded. "Where is she?"

"I don't know and I don't know," I said crossly, answering both his questions.

"She missed the bus!" he bellowed.

"I noticed," I grouched. "She forgot her package on the book rack so I picked it up."

"I bet she's back there looking for it," Jasper said. "You should have left it there."

"Obviously," I said. "But it's too late now. Didn't you say she worked at the grocery store in Granite Ridge? We can leave it there for her."

"She doesn't work there anymore," Jasper said. "Now look what you did."

He was right. I should have minded my own business, but if I had, the blond man would surely have stolen the present from the book rack. At least it was safe with me.

Chapter Three

GRANITE RIDGE IS NOT much more than a village, and Grandma lives north of it, on the road that once led to big logging camps but now leads nowhere in particular. The ridge itself is small, too. It's really a steep, rocky hill east of town, and on the other side of the hill you'll find Clayborne, the closest thing to a ghost town that I've ever seen. Clayborne is where you end up if you take the other road at Harper's Fork. I saw a lot of deserted old farms in the area when Gram took me for a ride there once. I kept thinking about that dreary place while the bus rushed us toward Granite Ridge. Jasper was right—it was the sort of place that Bugman would check out. And Bugman Jr. might want to check it out again over the next few days, especially if he went looking for Cissy so he could return her package.

"I have an idea," I said to Jasper, interrupting his bleak mood.

"Is it as stupid as your last one?" he asked crossly as he examined the hole in the knee of his jeans. His exploratory finger was making the hole bigger so I pulled his hand away. "Caroline, I wish you'd leave me alone," he told me. "And I wish you hadn't taken Cissy's package. What if she blames me?"

"She won't blame you," I said. "Stop making such a big deal over it. We'll ask about Cissy at the store. Someone will know where she lives and we can give Gram the package to take back for us. Maybe she'll drive over there this evening."

"Maybe," Jasper said doubtfully. "But Gram won't let me go along, I bet." He stood up suddenly and poked David's shoulder.

David turned around. "What's up, Jazz?"

"You can drive," Jasper stated. "Will you take me to Cissy Merchant's house so I can give her the package that Caroline took?"

David's eyes flickered to me, then back to Jasper, and I read his expression exactly. He had heard every word of The Great Package Debate, and he now lumped me in the same category with my cousin. Trouble with knobs on.

"She's Cissy Black now, since she got married," David said. "And I don't know where she lives. Anyway, your grandmother would have my hide if I took you someplace without asking her first. Why don't you do what Caroline says. Let your grandmother handle everything. That way you'll keep out of trouble for a change."

Jasper sank back in his seat, defeated. "Well, at least you can let me carry the package," he said to me. "I'll put it in my duffel bag. I've got lots of room."

I handed over the package, thankful to be rid of it. Maybe now he'll settle down, I told myself. A big mistake.

He shook the box. "It rattles," he announced.

"Leave the box alone before you break something," I told him. David glanced back over his shoulder, showing perfect teeth in a beautiful grin, and I was torn between adoring him because he was so gorgeous and hating him because he knew I was related to Jasper.

Jasper sniffed the package. "I smell cookies."

"You do not," I groaned. "The box has yards of wrapping paper on it. How could you smell anything?"

Jasper looked up at me over the crooked rims of his glasses. "I know what cookies smell like."

"I suppose." What's the use, I thought, and I pulled out my book again. Who was I to challenge the superior nose of Jasper Bugman Cartright?

Jasper stowed the package in his duffel bag, on top of his pajamas and what looked like a jar of grass and twigs. Believe me, I wasn't about to ask what lived in that jar.

After a while Jasper climbed into the empty seat in front of me and began pestering David about lottery tickets. When he found out that David didn't have any, he started in on the other passengers. The bus rolled along a narrow road lined with maples that spread dusty leaves above us. I yawned and turned a page. Jasper could have been worse. He often was.

* * *

"Granite Ridge!" the driver shouted, and I blinked awake again. David supervised Jasper, collecting his duffel bag and the world-renowned Bugman library. I followed them off the bus and across the parking lot to the Granite Ridge grocery store.

Where was Gram?

"I thought Gram was meeting us here," Jasper said.

"Maybe she's inside," David suggested, herding Jasper toward the store.

"But where's her truck?" Jasper asked loudly. I'd been wondering that myself.

"We'll see if Ben knows," David told Jasper. "Don't get yourself in an uproar."

I followed them inside—David held the screen door open for me—and Jasper ran to the counter in back where Ben, who owns the store, was waiting on a lady who looked familiar.

"Hey, Ben, where's Gram?" Jasper interrupted. "She was going to meet us here."

Ben smiled and nodded at me, then scowled faintly at Jasper. They haven't always seen eye to eye on things, and then there was the small matter of the snake that had escaped from Jasper and hid under the Bigbreak Cleaner display for three days.

"Your grandmother called five minutes ago, kids," Ben told us. "It seems that Mary Beth lost ten pounds worrying about her wedding and your grandma has to take in her dress before the ceremony tonight, so she's over at Mary Beth's place. She said you can wait here or let me drive you up the road when the store closes. Or," he added, eyeing David, "David here can use my car and take you home."

I looked at David and he looked at me. "Do you want to go now?" he asked.

"Sure. If you don't mind, that is." My heart was beating too fast.

"Yes!" Jasper shouted, spoiling the romantic moment. "David can take us."

"It's settled then," Ben responded. He handed his car keys to David and smiled at me once more. "It's nice to see you again, Caroline. You'll be going to Mary Beth's wedding, won't you? This here's her aunt, Florence Hooper."

"We've met before," Mrs. Hooper said. "Remember when your grandmother sent you over with some of her roses last month?"

"Sure," I told her. One of the curious things that goes on in small-town stores is this tendency customers have to hang around and talk. It's nice, but I was impatient to get going.

Mary Beth Hooper's Aunt Florence was in no hurry. "The wedding is going to be at my place," she went on. "Seven o'clock. You be sure to come. We're having dancing later for the young people and David will be there."

My interest increased sharply. I glanced at David and saw him looking at me again. "You don't want to miss it," he said.

"But I..." Jasper began.

Mrs. Hooper fixed him with an icy blue stare. "You're welcome, too, Jasper—if you leave all your specimens at home."

"Weddings..." Jasper began again, scowling, but suddenly he stopped. I could hear the wheels between his ears turning. "Weddings! Who did Cissy Merchant marry, Ben?"

"Somebody from around Clayborne," Ben said. "A man named Black. Why?"

"Do you know where she lives now?" Jasper asked. Good for him, I thought. I'd forgotten about Cissy and with good reason. The prospect of dancing with someone as good-looking as David could make a girl forget her own name.

Ben scowled and concentrated on the ceiling while he tried to refresh his memory. "Can't say I ever heard where Cissy lives these days," he said. Then he busied himself packing Mrs. Hooper's groceries into a sack.

Jasper looked up at me. "Now what are we going to do?"

"Don't panic," David told him. "Ben, does Cissy ever come in here?"

Ben shook his head. "Not since she quit and married that Peter Black."

"We'll find out where she is," David told Jasper. He put a big brown hand on Jasper's thin shoulder. "Let's get going. My folks are expecting me back pretty soon."

Jasper dutifully dragged The Collection and his duffel bag out the door, and I was right behind him, grateful that Ben didn't ask why Jasper was so curious about Cissy.

Gram lives less than a mile from the store, but it's a long walk on a hot afternoon if you're loaded down with luggage, so I was grateful that we had a ride. David got us there in minutes, and he carried Jasper's comic books and my tote to the porch. My cousin opened the door and I invited David inside. "Gram always has apple juice in the refrigerator."

David's slow, sweet grin raised goose bumps on me. "Thanks," he murmured, "But I have to get going. Are you going to the wedding tonight? Most of the town will be there and you'd have fun."

"I'd love to go," I told him. "But how can that many people dance at Mrs. Hooper's? I remember her house isn't that big."

"They'll be dancing outside, on the patio, on the deck, in the driveway, in the barn. You name it and there'll be a band and dancing going on there. Something for everybody. Even for a big-city girl."

It sounded like fun, but Gram hadn't told me about the wedding, so I was unprepared. "All I brought with me is jeans," I said.

He grinned and I felt as if I'd been plunged into stardust. "You're awfully cute just the way you are."

"Aw, for Pete's sake!" Jasper groaned.

David laughed and left, and I danced past Jasper on my way to the kitchen. "I thought you liked David."

"I do," he said. "But who cares about an old wedding. Or a dance. I'll stay here and read."

"We'll see," I said diplomatically as I poured myself cold apple juice. I couldn't imagine Gram letting him stay alone in the house.

Jasper took his belongings upstairs after announcing that he was moving into the back bedroom because it was his favorite. He said he could make a quick escape from Bugman's enemies by crawling out on the porch roof and jumping to the ground. I didn't care which room I had—both the upstairs bedrooms are tucked cozily under the roof with dormer windows looking out over the fields. The front bedroom also had a view of the road and a window seat. The window in the back bedroom was within reach of the potted flowers Gram puts on the porch roof each summer.

I drank my apple juice thirstily and would have taken my bag upstairs then, but the phone rang.

Gram was calling. "You're here. Good," she said. "I just spoke to Ben and he said David drove you home. You were lucky he was on the bus—you'd have been bored sitting in the store."

"How's the wedding dress coming along?" I asked her.

Gram laughed. "We'll have the dress finished in a little while if that girl doesn't lose another pound worrying about it. Look, Caroline, if I don't make it back by five-thirty, you and Jasper go ahead and eat. I left cold chicken for you."

"I saw it," I said. "Gram, do you think Cissy Merchant—or Black—will be coming to the wedding?"

"Cissy!" Gram exclaimed. "Whatever brought her to mind? I haven't seen her in—oh, weeks. And she lives near Clayborne now."

I explained the situation, omitting the part about the man who tried to take the package from me at the Harper's Fork bus depot. I'd tell Gram about that later, I decided. It didn't seem to be so awful, now that I was miles away. And it wasn't the sort of news anyone wants to dump on her grandmother over the phone.

"For heaven's sake," she marveled. "I wonder what Cissy was doing in Seattle. Wait and I'll ask our bride if she expects Cissy."

I hung on, listening to Gram as she talked to someone else. When she came back, she said, "Well, if this isn't the strangest thing, Caroline. Mary Beth saw Cissy three weeks ago and she invited her to the wedding, but Cissy said that she and her husband were moving away. Are you sure it was Cissy you saw?"

"Jasper talked to her. He says it was Cissy. I guess she came back."

"There'll be some people from Clayborne at the wedding," Gram told me. "I'll ask them tonight. We'll find Cissy and get the package back to her. Remind me about it if I forget."

Gram hung up then, and I carried my tote toward the stairs. I wanted a shower, if Jasper hadn't locked himself in the bathroom already.

But Jasper was sitting on the landing, his face white. He held a shoebox full of money on his lap.

"You took Cissy's money," he said. "Now what are we going to do?"

Chapter Four

I DROPPED MY TOTE and heard it roll down the stairs. My mind had gone so blank that if the roof had fallen on me, I wouldn't have noticed. I never saw so much money in my life! Quickly, before my legs gave out, I sat down on the steps.

"You shouldn't have opened the box," I croaked.

"I know," Jasper said. "But I wanted to see if it was really just cookies or something important, like maybe miracle medicine for Cissy that she has to have to keep from dying. Bugman would have—"

"Never mind Bugman!" I screamed. I yanked the box away from Jasper and he gave it up without a fight. "I thought you were sure this box had cookies in it!"

"It did." Jasper poked his glasses straight. "It had cookies on top of a piece of cardboard. And when I took out the cardboard, I saw the money. Do you think Cissy's called the police and told them about us?"

"She doesn't know we have the money." I put the lid back on the box. Maybe if I didn't look at it, I wouldn't be so scared, I thought. "But that man knows."

"What man?" Jasper asked.

I shouldn't have mentioned him. Jasper would really be scared if he knew how the man tried to take the box from me at Harper's Fork. The money had to be the reason the man wanted the package. "Listen, Jasper," I said hastily, "Let's put the cookies back and wrap the box up again so that no one will know you opened it."

"Maybe we won't have to go to jail then," Jasper said.

"Don't be silly. We won't go to jail." But I wasn't all that certain. Why hadn't I left the stupid box right where it was, on top of the book rack in the bus depot!

But what about Jasper? He hadn't wasted any time snooping in Cissy's package. We seemed to go from bad to worse with no stops in between where we could think things over.

I hustled Jasper back to his room. The wrapping paper lay on his bed with the tangled ribbons. A square of cardboard stacked with cookies sat on the floor.

I handed him the box. "Put the cookies back just like you found them. I'll see what I can do with the wrapping paper."

We worked quickly, silently, until the package was wrapped up again. It didn't look too bad, but anyone who examined it closely would know that it had been opened. That was a problem I'd deal with when I had to.

"Gram says she'll ask around at the wedding tonight and see if someone knows where Cissy is," I told Jasper.

He nodded soberly. "Gram's going to kill us when she finds out what's in the package," he predicted.

I don't believe in encouraging little kids to lie, but this seemed like one of those occasions when total disclosure would lead straight to total disaster. "Let's not tell," I said suddenly. "It would only worry Gram. This way, she'll find out where Cissy is and get the package back to her, and that will be the end of it." And, I thought, we'd be spared dozens of questions and a mountain of advice about minding our own business. If Gram found out everything, we'd hear about it for a year.

"I bet Cissy is really worried about her money," Jasper said after a long silence. "Maybe it's her life savings."

"I doubt it." I'd been thinking hard during that long silence. Who wraps up money in a shoebox, making it look like a present? Sure, people give money as gifts, but not that much. Not in cash. I'd write a check instead, just in case the box was lost. Any normal person would.

But there must have been thousands and thousands of dollars in the box, because I'd seen only hundred-dollar bills in it. At least two dozen stacks of them.

Stacks of hundred-dollar bills that someone wanted to move from one place to another. So someone had hidden them in wrapping paper

—kids' wrapping paper printed with balloons and kittens and big pink flags that said "Happy Birthday."

I had an awful feeling that things were more complicated than I knew.

"It'll be all right," I said staunchly. I hoped I was right.

Gram came home half an hour later. Jasper and I were in the kitchen, silently getting ready for dinner. He'd set the table and I was nearly finished making a big salad when her old truck roared in the driveway, backfired, and stopped. Jasper and I stared at each other as Gram opened the front door and hurried down the hall to the kitchen. I winked and grinned, hoping to cheer him up.

"Hi, kids! Oh, good, you made salad." Gram kissed me and hugged Jasper hard enough to make him squeak. She was taller than I and lean as a stick, and her gray hair curled tightly around her face. She was wearing a dress instead of her usual jeans, and she saw me taking note of it.

"I thought I'd better practice wearing a skirt before tonight," she said. She took the chicken out of the refrigerator and passed a bottle of milk to Jasper. "Here, Jazz, you pour. And try to hit the holes in the glasses, okay?"

Some of the tension that had been holding me up leaked away and my knees began to shake. I put the salad on the table, hoping Gram didn't notice the shape I was in. "I didn't bring a dress, Gram," I said, after clearing my throat. "Will they let me come tonight?"

"Certainly. They'll even let Jasper come,

comic books and all." Gram watched Jasper pour three glasses of milk, and nodded in satisfaction when he only spilled a few drops. "Is everything all right, Jazz?" she asked. "You're so quiet."

Jasper opened his mouth and shut it without speaking.

"It was a long bus trip," I said quickly.

"Aw." Gram tousled Jasper's hair. "You'll feel better after you eat."

But she was the only one with an appetite. I could barely swallow and Jasper gave up after half-a-dozen bites. Gram didn't seem to notice, though. She chatted busily about the wedding dress, the groom—who worked in the hardware store at Harper's Fork—and the three bands that were going to play at the reception after the wedding. It would be the biggest wedding Granite Ridge had ever seen, she told us.

I tried to pretend enthusiasm, but I was worried that she'd remember Cissy's package and ask to see it. When the meal ended, at long last, I leaped up to clear the table and Jasper disappeared in the direction of his bedroom.

"He seems off his feed," Gram observed as she put the leftover chicken back in the refrigerator.

"He'll be himself tomorrow," I said. At that moment, I would have welcomed Jasper's usual crisis-a-minute behavior, because that would mean that he didn't have a worry in the world. And in order for Jasper not to have a worry, the package was going to have to disappear from Gram's house and reappear in Cissy's lap, wherever she was, by magic. As things stood, we didn't have a wishing star between us.

What we did have was Cissy's package, hidden under Jasper's bed.

I wished I had someone to talk to. I needed someone to help me make plans. Someone to help me, period. That awful man back at Harper's Fork knew I had the box. What if he found me before we found Cissy? I was beginning to think that maybe we'd be better off telling Gram the whole thing, letting her straighten it out, and then resigning ourselves to listening to her and our parents fuss about it until they thought we'd learned a good lesson. What an awful choice to have to make!

"How do you like David?" Gram asked me.

"What? Oh, David," I babbled. "He seems nice."

Gram loaded the dishwasher while she talked. "David's folks own the big dairy ranch out on Valley Road. You probably know the one I mean. His mother made the bridesmaids' dresses and that was a big job for her to take on, especially now that they have a boarder. And David's little sisters are a handful and a half, let me tell you."

"Umm," I mumbled as I wiped off the table with a damp cloth.

"They're going to miss David when he goes away to college," Gram said.

I looked up. "He's that old?"

"He'll go next year. He'll be a senior at North County High now."

Any other time I would have been eager to hear about someone like David. Now, though, I had more pressing problems.

We finished in the kitchen and Gram hurried away to put on the dress she was going to wear to the wedding. If she hadn't been so distracted, she probably would have noticed that I was having a hard time keeping my smile from looking glued on. I was grateful that Mary Beth Hooper had decided to get married on that particular night. Otherwise Gram, an expert at reading minds and digging up secrets, would have had the whole thing out of me in a minute. I didn't relish the thought of explaining that the "present" we were trying to return was something else entirely. And maybe the police were looking for us. Or the blond man. Or both.

But as I climbed the stairs, I considered blabbing the whole thing and getting it over with. No matter what Gram did to us, at least we'd have someone on our side after she finished yelling.

I rejected the idea hastily. Maybe after the wedding, when Gram wasn't so busy, she'd be less likely to worry. The awful truth was that I didn't want to tell her or anyone, even though keeping quiet left me with a guilty conscience that turned the chicken I'd eaten to stone. I just wanted to get the package back to Cissy and forget about it.

Jasper was sitting on the floor in his room, examining whatever lived in the jar he'd brought with him from Seattle. When he saw me looking in his open door, he screwed the lid back on. "Did she say anything?" he asked.

"She's so busy she forgot," I told him. "Do you have another pair of jeans? We're going to be leaving in a few minutes, and those jeans look like they were chewed by bears." The hole in the knee was now at least three inches wide.

"Where are we going?"

"To the wedding. Don't pretend you don't remember. If I were you, I wouldn't do anything to aggravate Gram now."

Jasper set his jaw stubbornly. "I don't want to go to any old wedding. Anyway, I'm sick to my stomach."

"She'll know something's up."

"Well, I wasn't the one who took Cissy's money!" he argued.

"You were the one who found out it *was* money," I pointed out.

He fidgeted. "I've been thinking," he said finally.

Experience taught me that Jasper's thinking often caused a lot more problems than expected. Warily, I asked, "Thinking about what?"

"Cissy wouldn't have left this box in the depot if she knew it had money in it," he said. "I wouldn't."

I considered his observation. It made sense. No one would let that much money out of her hands, even for an instant. "Maybe she wasn't giving that present to someone," I said slowly. "Maybe someone gave it to her."

Jasper nodded. "So she just forgot the box, and she wouldn't bother calling the police over what was maybe only cookies."

"Or shoes," I said.

Jasper poked his glasses. "Maybe nobody will be mad."

I sat down on his bed. "Maybe nobody has to know anything," I said, a new idea dawning. "We could keep the box here until Dad drives us home. We'll ask him to stop at the depot in

Harper's Fork and I'll put the box back where I found it. Then it won't be our problem anymore!"

"Would Uncle Ted do that?" Jasper asked. "Would he stop if you didn't tell him why?"

"No." I frowned, thinking so hard that my head ached. "Listen, don't worry about it. I'll think of something to tell him when the time comes."

We could hear Gram's bedroom door open and close downstairs. Jasper sucked in his breath. "What if she remembers about the package? What if she finds out where Cissy lives and wants to take the package back?"

"Then we'll let her. One way or another, we'll get rid of it and no one will have to find out that we knew about the money."

Jasper sagged with relief. "You really think everything is going to be all right?"

I nodded briskly. "Now, forget about it. Did you bring another pair of jeans?"

"No. Why do I need other jeans?"

Groaning, I left the room. I spent three quick minutes upstairs, changing out of the red vest and white shirt I'd been wearing all day and pulling on a pale yellow shirt. That was the best I could do. On my way downstairs, I fluffed up my hair with my fingers and hoped I looked acceptable.

Gram looked magnificent. She was even wearing the rose quartz beads I'd given her last winter on her sixtieth birthday. And Jasper honored the occasion by washing his hands and face—I noticed the moment he came downstairs. He was trying hard not to annoy Gram.

"Are we ready?" Gram asked.

"Ready," we said.

We closed the door behind us and piled into Gram's ancient pickup truck. I asked if I could drive the short distance to Mrs. Hooper's but Gram told me that there was no point in tempting fate. Granite Ridge was too small to have a police force and also too small to have any crime, but it would be just our luck, Gram said, to have the county police pass us on the road. I didn't argue. The last thing in the world I wanted to do was attract the attention of the county police. There was always the chance that Jasper and I were wrong and Cissy did know what was in the box and who had taken it.

It was nicer, I decided, to look forward to an evening dancing with David than an evening worrying about things we couldn't do anything about anyway.

Chapter Five

I DISCOVERED THAT the wedding was going to be sweet and different. The minister and the bridal party would stand on the porch, which had been decorated with flowers and ferns, while everyone else watched from the long, sloping lawn. There were a few chairs up front for the older people, and I had to wrestle Jasper out of one of them and pull him down the path to the end of the lawn, next to a row of late-blooming roses.

David got up from where he was sitting with some other kids his age and joined us, folding up his long legs gracefully and sitting between Jasper and me.

"I was afraid you'd change your mind," he whispered.

"I love weddings," I whispered back.

"Oh, glop," Jasper growled. He fished around under his shirt and pulled out a dog-eared comic book. "David, have you read this one?"

David examined the Bugman comic seriously. "No, I haven't. Maybe you could let me borrow it."

Jasper clutched the comic book in panic. "You can come over to Gram's and read it."

That was all right with me, and apparently it was all right with David, too. "How about tomorrow?" he asked me.

"Jasper isn't doing anything tomorrow," I said. "Sure, you come on over."

David grinned and tilted one broad shoulder down toward me. "I could bring along my sisters. They'd love to know Jasper better."

But Jasper overheard that. "No girls!" he pronounced.

Before I could protest, the musicians standing beside the porch began playing, and the bridesmaids walked around the corner of the house and climbed the steps. The groom blushed as the bride followed her friends and stood next to him. The service began and I smiled all the way through it.

When it ended, the people on the lawn let loose pink and white balloons and everyone clapped wildly. Even Jasper liked that part. The musicians played while the bride and groom walked around the house to the patio where their wedding cake sat in the center of a long table. We followed and David took my hand. Jasper pretended he didn't notice.

After the cake was cut and distributed, the table was moved off the patio and the bride and groom danced to a waltz. Other people from the wedding party joined them, and the sight was so pretty I had tears in my eyes.

"Would you like to waltz?" David asked. "Or shall we go dance to one of the other bands?"

I heard faint music coming from the front of the house, more slow-dancing tunes. Then, from the other side of the big barn south of the house, a rock band started up, and most of the teenagers in the crowd surged in that direction.

"I think I'm dressed for that music," I told David, but as he led me away, I looked back at the patio where the bridal party dipped and twirled, and I wished that I'd brought a dress with me. And even though David looked nice in tan slacks and a sport coat, we would have been out of place with the men wearing tuxedos and women in fancy dresses. Another time, I thought, sighing to myself.

The rock band was good and we danced on close-clipped grass, barefoot and happy. David shed his jacket and loosened his tie, and no one paid any attention to the city girl in jeans.

And I didn't pay any attention to Jasper. We danced for an hour before I remembered that I'd come with Gram and Jasper and hadn't seen either of them since the ceremony.

"I'd better go find Jasper," I told David breathlessly. "He's probably pestering someone."

David slung his arm around my shoulders as we walked back to the house. The sun was setting, and above us the sky reached beyond forever, deep blue and streaked with crimson.

"Wait," David whispered suddenly, and he pulled me under a willow tree that drooped graceful branches clear to the grass.

He lifted my chin with his fingers and

looked at me for a long time. Then he kissed me, quickly, shyly, as if he wasn't certain I would like it. But I did.

"You're pretty, you know that?" he said softly.

He embarrassed me and I hid my face against his shoulder. "I think we'd better look for Jasper."

"Are you mad?" he asked, worried.

I shook my head, and just to prove it to him I kissed him—just as quickly and shyly.

Both of us laughed then, and he pulled me out from under the willow. We walked hand in hand and I forgot all about Cissy's package, the money, and the man in the depot. I almost forgot about Jasper—but not quite.

Jasper wasn't with Gram. She was busy serving coffee, and she said she'd thought he was with me.

Oh, great. "He's around somewhere," I said, but I had a hunch he wasn't.

"Some of the youngsters are sitting out by the driveway," another woman said, and David and I walked in that direction.

We'd just about given up when David saw Jasper and pointed him out to me. "See? He's over there, talking to our boarder."

I winced. Jasper had cornered a young man and was showing him the Bugman comic book. The young man pretended a serious interest in it, but I saw him glancing around, as if he were hoping to be interrupted.

"We'd better rescue your boarder—he must be miserable," I said.

David only laughed. "I think Jasper has finally found one of his own. Mike works for the forestry service and he's been here for weeks looking for gypsy moths. Bugs."

To my horror, Jasper pulled out the paper sack containing his cocoons and shared the grisly collection with his newfound friend. "I've got to put a stop to this," I whispered. "Next thing, he'll be showing off his world-famous assortment of old lottery tickets. Or telling all the family secrets. I don't know which would be worse."

I reached Jasper just as David's boarder was holding up one of the cocoons. ". . . lepidopterous," he was saying. "The way you can tell is— Hello. Who's this?" He smiled at me as David introduced us, and he kept on smiling even when David explained that I was Jasper's cousin.

"I was telling Jasper here about how to identify his cocoons," Mike Slattery told me. He didn't look like someone who spent his time searching the woods for gypsy moths—his skin was too pale. Actually, he looked like a kid I knew who spent all his time hanging around bowling alleys watching people. He had hard, narrow eyes, too. Creepy.

"I hope you haven't been bothering Mr. Slattery," I said to Jasper.

"I haven't been bothering anybody!" Jasper howled. "Why do you always say things like that?"

Mike Slattery held up one hand in protest. "We've been having a great conversation," he said. "Jasper seems to know every inch of the woods around here."

"I can help you look for gypsy moths," Jasper said with an ingratiating smile.

"You know you aren't supposed to go in the woods anymore," I reminded him.

"Why is that?" Mr. Slattery asked me quickly. Something in his eyes changed and I was sure he didn't really want to be Jasper's friend.

But I was Jasper's cousin, so I wasn't going to tell about his adventures with the angry farmer on the other side of the ridge. "People have been firing guns in the woods this summer, so we aren't supposed to walk there," I told Mr. Slattery.

"Mike knows about that," David said. "We warned him when he came that the woods aren't safe anymore."

"I'm careful," Mr. Slattery said. "Did you ever see any of those people, Caroline?"

"I never go in the woods," I told him shortly. He was too curious.

"Who do you suppose they are?" David asked Mike.

"I have no idea," Mr. Slattery said. A scowl flickered across his face and disappeared. "Probably the shots are just target practice. Some guys are very serious about getting ready for hunting season. Say, Jasper, how about showing me the lottery tickets you told me about?"

He wasn't interested in Jasper's grubby collection—he just wanted to change the subject—but I decided to let them alone. Jasper exasperated me and I didn't like Mike Slattery very much. Definitely, he was the type who would sneak up on an unsuspecting gypsy moth and do whatever forestry service people do to moths when they catch them. Ugh. Also, he bothered me because he liked to ask questions but didn't want to answer any.

David and I went back to report to Gram that all was well with Jasper, and then we walked over to the driveway to watch the dancing there. David slipped his arm around me while we stood outside the circle of lanterns that illuminated the driveway. The evening was warm and sweet-scented with late summer roses. I thought during those delicious moments that I wouldn't have minded standing there forever.

And then I saw him—the heavyset blond man from the depot at Harper's Fork. He stood across the driveway from us, close to one of the lanterns. The light shone directly on his mean, pouchy face as he watched the dancers closely. And I knew without a doubt that he was looking for me.

I stepped back into the dark, holding my breath. My heart was beating so hard that I was sure everyone could hear it.

"What's wrong?" David asked.

I backed up even farther. "I have to go home," I whispered. I wanted to run to Gram's house, lock the door behind me, and hide under the bed. I was so scared I saw spots in front of my eyes.

"But why? The dancing will go on until midnight. And your grandmother won't mind if you stay."

"Please," I whispered, my gaze fixed on the man across the driveway. "Tell Gram and Jasper that I left."

"Hey, what's going on?"

"I have to go. Right now." I didn't know what

would happen if the man saw me, and I didn't want to wait to find out.

David followed me as I blundered across the dark lawn. "What's wrong? Are you mad at me?"

"No, of course not."

"Then let me drive you."

"It's so close that I'll be home almost as fast if I walk." I looked back and couldn't see the man. What if he was creeping across the lawn in the dark?

I took off running but David was right behind me. "You don't have to come with me," I told him over my shoulder.

"You can't stop me," he said. "You're fast but I'm faster." He grabbed my hand, slowing me down. "Tell me what scared you."

We walked close together, and even though I was listening hard, I couldn't hear anything but our footsteps in the soft dirt at the side of the road. I wanted to tell him everything, even about the money, but I didn't dare. I didn't know him well enough—maybe he'd go straight to Gram. Or the police. Or Cissy. Or maybe he knew the blond man.

"Did you know everyone at the wedding?" I asked.

"Do you always answer questions with questions?" he retaliated. "Okay, I'll start. No, I didn't know all the people there. Not even half of them."

"Did you see that man standing across the driveway from us? The big blond man, sort of fat?"

David shook his head. "I'm not sure I remember who you mean, but the only people I knew were dancing, not standing around watching. What about this man? Is he the one who scared you?"

I took a chance. "I saw him at the depot in Harper's Fork. He...tried to get friendly." There. That wasn't the truth, but it would do.

David squeezed my hand. "I think I know what you mean. What a creep. Look, Caroline, you're awfully pretty and there are a lot of strange guys who will want to get acquainted with you. But you don't have anything to worry about now. I'm with you."

I didn't have the heart to tell David that I was sure I could have handled a man who was only trying to flirt. What I wasn't sure I could handle was a man who wanted the money Cissy had lost. A man who wouldn't take a brisk no for an answer.

Chapter Six

DAVID STAYED WITH me until Gram and Jasper got home about an hour later. We sat in the kitchen drinking apple juice and stuffing ourselves with cookies, and learning enough about each other to discover that we could be a lot more than just friends. But I was listening not only to what David said but also to the night sounds outside. And I didn't feel safe until Gram's truck roared up.

David promised Jasper that he'd come back the next day at eleven to take us down the old logging road to a pond in the woods where there was a perfect place for a picnic.

"Are you sure you want *Caroline?*" Jasper asked. "She hates the woods."

"I do not," I argued. Actually I wasn't too crazy about woods, but going on a picnic with David was worth all sorts of inconvenience—even Jasper tagging along.

After David went home, Gram didn't comment on our leaving the wedding reception without saying goodbye. But Jasper said, "We knew you'd run off with David so no one else could talk to him."

"Jasper, brush your teeth and go to bed," Gram said. She was laughing. I longed to tell her everything and maybe I would have, right then, if she hadn't gone off to her room, still laughing. Somehow I couldn't run after her and pour out the whole story, including the uncomfortable fact that I had been withholding important information. That's like lying. Gram would hate that.

It was a long night. I'd never noticed before how many different noises there are around Gram's house. Each time a night bird cried I sat up in bed, clutching the blankets and ready to scream. When dawn came I was so tired that I fell asleep in spite of being worried.

Gram let me sleep until an hour before David was due. At the kitchen table I saw that Jasper hadn't slept well either, for his blue eyes looked tired and his face was pale. He kept a Bugman comic next to his place and read it while he ate.

I gobbled my food, scared that Gram would remember to ask about the package. She didn't, and I began to believe that maybe, just maybe, she had forgotten to ask about Cissy at the wedding the night before.

Jasper and I finished breakfast while Gram gossiped on the phone about the wedding. When we were on our way upstairs to dress, Jasper whispered to me, "Should I bring the present when we go on the picnic?"

"Of course not!" I hissed. "Leave it where it is."

"But what if Gram finds it?"

We paused outside Jasper's door to think.

"I know!" Jasper whispered. "I'll put it out on the porch roof."

I shook my head. "She might water the flowers in the pots out there." I couldn't bear the thought of Gram finding the money accidentally. This was getting worse and worse!

Jasper looked bleak. "I better take it."

Maybe he was right. "Okay," I said. "Put it in your duffel bag and throw some of your comics in on top of it."

Jasper gave me a pained look. "That's what I was going to do, Caroline."

I gave him a gentle shove. "Go get ready."

When David arrived, I had dressed in my jeans, white shirt, and red vest again, and Jasper was wearing his new-but-already-ruined jeans and a shirt that said "Bugman Victorious!" on the front. Gram contributed cookies and lemonade, which I carried, and Jasper had his duffel bag slung over one shoulder and an innocent expression on his face.

"Are you ready?" David asked. He carried a wicker picnic basket and a folded blanket.

"Yes, but I hope we aren't going very far," I told him. "That basket looks heavy."

"It's a short walk," he said. "You're going to like this place."

Just then I noticed Gram, standing behind Jasper and studying the duffel bag with a puzzled look.

"We'd better get started," I said hurriedly. This was no time for Gram to be curious about the duffel bag. "Come on, Jasper." I looked at Gram and nodded toward the duffel. "Bugman travels everywhere," I said to her. She winked at me and nodded solemnly at Jasper.

Jasper bolted out the door, putting distance between Gram and our secret, and I breathed deeply. "We'll see you later, Gram."

She waved goodbye and we started off down the old logging road, David and I walking side by side and Jasper leaping and bounding all around us like a rabbit. Fireweed was going to seed on both sides of the road, and when Jasper ran through the stalks, he scattered the cottony seeds into the air. They blew around us, then sailed off, ahead of the late summer wind that carried the scent of autumn with it.

We turned three bends in the road and then David led us off on a narrow path nearly overgrown with ferns. "Here," he said, pushing past a huckleberry bush. "Here's the pond."

"Yea!" Jasper yelled, dropping his duffel bag where he stood and running toward the water. Two ducks flew up, squawking angrily.

"Is he always like this?" David asked.

"Gee," I said, "I thought he was being especially quiet today."

David saw me grinning. "Well, at least he brought along some stuff to keep himself occupied. I take it he has good old Bugman in the duffel bag?"

"Yes." I spread out the blanket on the warm, dry grass.

David sat down on a log and I poured lemonade into paper cups. I'd just tasted mine when Jasper came panting up.

"Look what I found!" he exclaimed, holding out his palm. A dirty old lottery ticket.

"There's garbage everywhere," I said philosophically while Jasper stuck the ticket in his pocket. "How many does that make?"

Without taking them out to count, Jasper said, "I found eighteen this week and one has a square that hasn't been scratched yet. Last week I found twenty and Buddy Clausen only found fourteen."

"This is some sort of contest?" David asked, fascinated.

"Sure," Jasper said proudly. "Every week we collect used lottery tickets and whoever gets the most gets to keep the tarantula for the next week."

Now I knew what was in the jar full of grass and twigs.

"You want to see it, David?" Jasper asked, but David was spared because Mike Slattery walked in off the road, with a backpack and several little orange cardboard boxes dangling from cords.

"I thought I heard my friend Jasper," he said.

"Hey, Mike!" Jasper yelled. "What are you doing out here?"

Mr. Slattery held up one of the cardboard boxes. "Gathering my traps. I've got them scattered all over the woods, and today's the day I take them back in to see what I caught."

"Gypsy moths?" Jasper asked, excited.

Mr. Slattery shook his head. "I hope not. They're bad news, because they kill fir trees. If the traps are empty, we'll hope that means there aren't any gypsy moths in the area and we don't have to spray the woods."

"Can I look?" Jasper asked, reaching for one of the boxes, but Mr. Slattery whisked it out of reach.

"This is official business, Jasper," he said. He looked around, too curious to suit me. "Having a picnic?"

"Sure. There's plenty to eat, so do you want to join us?" David asked.

"No, thanks. Got to get moving." Mr. Slattery nodded to me and walked back toward the road. "See you guys!" he called back.

"I could go with Mike," Jasper grumbled.

"No, you can't," David said briskly, handing Jasper his lemonade. "Mike has to go up on the ridge, too, and you know what your grandmother would do to you if she heard about that."

"There's nobody shooting up there anymore," Jasper said. "I asked some of the kids at the wedding last night, and they said the shooting stopped."

But a few minutes later a shot rang out, echoing along the ridge and scaring all of us.

David's mouth tightened. "That sounded close."

"You don't suppose it's someone hunting, do you?" I asked.

"This isn't hunting season," David said grimly. He was looking off toward the ridge, shaking his head slowly.

"What's wrong?" I asked.

"I hope Mike is all right," he said. "Maybe I'd better go have a look. He walked in that direction."

"We'll go, too," I said. I didn't really want to, but I didn't want to stay behind at the pond, either.

Jasper grabbed up his duffel bag, but David and I left our stuff behind. We marched straight down the road until it gave out and then we followed a trail off to the right that wound back through the woods toward the ridge.

Another shot rang out and Jasper flinched. David stood very still, listening. "It's hard to tell where the sound comes from," he said.

Once more the woods seemed to rip apart with a deafening shot and David motioned to us to lie flat. I was sure we were about to be killed.

Several shots rang out close together and, incredibly, we heard men laughing. Instantly, David was on his feet.

"Hey! Hey, you morons! Stop shooting! There are people in the woods! Stop shooting!"

Silence. All we could hear was the wind stirring in the tops of the firs.

"Don't shoot!" David yelled again.

Silence.

We turned and ran, David pulling Jasper along and me sprinting behind. We ran back to the pond and stood staring at each other for a long minute.

"We'd better tell someone," I gasped finally. "Mike Slattery could be hurt."

"That's what I'm afraid of."

"Did you see anything?" I asked. "I was too scared to look."

David shook his head. "I didn't see a thing."

"I did," Jasper said in a small, thin voice. He

shoved his glasses straight. "I saw a man watching us."

David stared at him. "Where? What man?"

Jasper pointed back to where we'd been. "Up there," he said. "Before you made us lie down. I saw a man wearing camouflage clothes. He had a red band on his sleeve. And he had a rifle."

"Did he see us?" David said urgently.

Jasper took a deep breath. "I think so."

David chewed his lip and scowled. "Well, we can't stay here, but we'd probably better not go back by the road."

"How, then?" I asked, scared.

"If we go through the woods on this side of the road, we'll come out west of town, but that's all right. It's better than getting shot."

We gathered up the picnic things and were ready to go when we heard voices on the road. David motioned us down again, and Jasper and I huddled together behind a tangle of brambles while David crouched behind a tree. Three men walked up close to the pond and looked around. All three wore rumpled uniforms of some sort, marked with splotches of brown and green. Each wore a black beret, each had a piece of red cloth tied to one arm—and one of them was the blond man from the depot in Harper's Fork.

"I told you that you'd scare them off," one man said roughly. "You and your damned fool games."

I closed my eyes and bit the back of my hand to keep from crying. Brush crackled, the men laughed and walked away.

I let out the breath I'd been holding. Jasper

whispered, "That was him, the guy who was watching us."

"Which one?" I whispered back.

"The fat blond one."

The man from the depot.

"Never mind," I said. "He didn't see us this time."

If we were lucky, there wouldn't be a next time.

Chapter Seven

I WAS TOO SCARED to think straight at that point. The blond man seemed to be everywhere—and I knew he wanted the present. I was tempted to grab Jasper's duffel bag, run after the man, and throw it at him. That would end our problems.

But would it? What if Cissy found out we had taken the package she had stupidly left behind? She could accuse us of stealing it, and who would believe that we'd be dumb enough to hand it over to a man we didn't even know? Who would believe us about anything? We'd done everything wrong and nothing right. Why hadn't I told Gram when Jasper found the money? We'd waited so long that now she might think we wanted to keep it. She was going to be furious, but that didn't matter anymore. We needed help.

As we got to our feet, I whispered urgently to Jasper. "Listen, we're going to tell Gram as soon as we get back to the house. We've got to have help from someone."

"She'll kill us," Jasper whispered, panicked. "She'll call our folks."

"I'd rather be bawled out than shot," I hissed.

David eased out from behind the tree, watching the path where the men had disappeared. He still looked astonished.

"Who were they?" I asked when he got close enough so I didn't have to raise my voice.

"I don't know," David said. "I never saw any of them before. They must be from the old farm on the other side of the ridge. But why the uniforms? And why are they over on this side? Did you get a look at their guns?"

I knew David didn't expect answers to all those questions—he was just asking to hear himself talk, and I was grateful for that, because I might have been able to answer one of the questions. The men were on this side of the ridge looking for me.

"Do you think they're gone now?" Jasper asked.

"It sounded like they went back the way they came," David said. "We'll have a look out on the road, and if they're nowhere in sight, we can run back quick."

"Some picnic," I said, laughing shakily. "What did you do with the basket and the blanket?"

"I tossed 'em in that direction," David told me, pointing to thick brush not far from where he'd been hiding.

"Let's grab the stuff and get going," I said

nervously. "The men might decide to come back."

We found the basket on its side and the blanket lying in a heap near by. Jasper fidgeted behind us as we made our way back to the road—I could tell he wasn't very anxious to get out in the open where we could be seen.

Then we heard footsteps coming down the road from the ridge. We sank down quickly, holding our breaths. Whoever was coming wasn't making any effort to be quiet—but then I wouldn't either, if I were carrying a gun.

David raised his head cautiously. "It's Mike!" he said aloud. "He's all right!"

We got to our feet and scrambled after David, who'd run out to the road. Mike Slattery didn't seem surprised to see us.

"Run out of food already?" he asked David, but he was looking at me. Even while his mouth smiled, his eyes searched me, took note of the dust on my clothes and the scratches on my bare arms. I didn't know how David and Jasper could like him—I sure didn't. He really gave me the creeps.

"The picnic got canceled by gunfire," David said, laughing a little. "Hey, Mike, we were worried about you. Those guys in the uniforms were right around where you were picking up your traps."

I saw that Mike had even more cardboard traps now. "They weren't anywhere near me," he said. "Those idiots—someday they're going to hit someone."

"But who are they?" David asked. "We got a good look at three of them and I've never seen them around here before. And those uniforms! They looked like something out of a TV show."

"They're probably just guys from the city, out here for target practice on weekends," Mike said, shrugging as if he didn't care. Or didn't think they were dangerous. "Gotta get back, folks, and have a look in the traps."

David walked in step with him, but Jasper and I straggled behind, and Jasper kept looking back over his shoulder. I would have, too, but I was too scared. Sometimes it doesn't pay to look behind you because you might not like what's following you.

I didn't believe a word Mike said. Those men weren't out here for target practice and he knew it.

Jasper grabbed my hand and yanked on it until I stopped to hear what he had to say. "Maybe we should tell Mike," he whispered. "Maybe he could help."

"No!" I answered in a panic. "Don't tell anyone but Gram. It has to be a secret."

We hurried a little to catch up to the others, and I could tell that Jasper was obeying me only because he was too scared to do anything else. He kept looking back—and I kept expecting to hear shots again, or footsteps running behind us and voices yelling for us to stop and hand over the duffel bag.

But nothing happened, except that we covered the distance between the pond and Gram's house in half the time it had taken us before.

Mike walked on ahead, leaving David standing by Gram's gate. "Sorry about all this," David said. "I don't suppose you'd want to have a picnic in your grandmother's yard where you'd be safe from those jerks back on the ridge?"

"Don't talk about food," Jasper groaned, and he did look sick.

"I think we'll have to take a raincheck on the picnic," I told David. I had a hunch he was more than willing to go home. "I'm not very hungry now, either."

David looked politely disappointed. "Maybe tomorrow," he said. "I'm going to tell my dad about those guys we saw. I think they're dangerous, even if Mike doesn't."

I was so relieved I even found the courage to smile. "So do I," I told him. "Those uniforms—that was scary."

"I suppose it makes them feel like they're better shots than they really are, dressing up like that," David said.

"They're paramilitary survivalists," Jasper said suddenly. "Phony soldiers." His anxious, pale face was streaked with dirt and his glasses were hanging crooked again. "Bugman had to fight them once, when they were trying to take over our government. That paramilitary outfit had all kinds of guns and bombs, and real tanks, even. They wore uniforms just like that."

David rumpled Jasper's hair. "That was in a comic book," he told him. "Things like that don't happen in places like Granite Ridge."

"But . . ." Jasper began.

"Don't worry about it," David said. "You'll spoil your vacation because of some dumb guys who were shooting up the woods just for fun."

"But you were scared, too!" Jasper cried defiantly.

"Sure I was," David agreed. "I don't want to be shot by accident any more than I want to be shot on purpose."

"But you hid from them!" Jasper persisted.

"You bet I did," David said. He closed one big brown hand over Jasper's thin shoulder and shook it gently. "That's instinct. But I don't want you to worry about anything now. I'll tell my dad and he'll talk to the county police. They'll put a stop to whatever those guys are doing."

"But they couldn't find them last month!" Jasper argued. "They looked and the men were gone, and the guys at the old farm said they didn't know who'd been up on the ridge but it wasn't them."

"The police will sort it out," David declared confidently. He couldn't know that Jasper and I hoped the police wouldn't sort everything out.

We said goodbye and Jasper and I went inside the house. I had a big knot in my stomach—telling Gram about the money was at the very bottom of my list of fun things to do in Granite Ridge.

But Gram wasn't home. We found a note on the table, telling us that she was visiting someone named Nan Kelper, who was home with her new baby.

"Do you know Nan Kelper?" I asked Jasper. He seemed to know everything about the town, and we needed to talk to Gram fast.

"I've heard of her, but I don't know her." He was hugging his duffel bag to his chest.

"I'll look in the phone book," I told him. "You get yourself something to eat from the refrigerator."

"I'm not hungry," he said.

"Then get out the lemonade and pour us some of that. I'm thirsty." I was busy with the thin little phone book Gram kept on a shelf next to the phone. Kelper. Kelper. I couldn't find a listing for anyone named Kelper, but this Nan must live nearby because Gram had walked to visit her. I'd seen Gram's old truck in the driveway when we came home.

I could call David's house and ask someone there for the Kelper number. They'd understand that Jasper and I didn't want to be alone right now. I found the number and dialed it. Busy signal.

Jasper poured lemonade for us, getting most of it in the glasses and very little on the counter. We sat at the table silently, drinking one glass of lemonade after another until the pitcher was empty, while Jasper fiddled with his lottery tickets. I tried David's number over and over, but the line was always busy.

Jasper put his head down on his arms. His grubby fists were clenched, as if he were ready to fight an enemy. The duffel bag was next to his chair.

"Jasper, why don't you go upstairs and have a nap," I said. "I'll keep trying to find Gram, and I'll let you know as soon as I do."

To my surprise, he got up and started for the stairs, dragging the duffel bag with him. "Promise you'll call me when you find Gram."

I promised faithfully, even as I dialed David's number again. Still busy.

There must be someone else I could call for Nan Kelper's number, I thought, but I knew very few people in Granite Ridge, and explanations have a way of getting out of hand. By the time I'd finished telling someone who was practically a total stranger that I needed to talk to Gram, that stranger would be wondering why a nearly grown-up person needed her grandmother that much. The whole town might find out that Caroline Cartright was in some sort of trouble, and I didn't know who I could trust.

And there was one person who worried me. Mike Slattery—who boarded at David's house. I sat down heavily, as if all my breath had been knocked out of me. What if he answered the phone? It would be better if Mike didn't know Jasper and I were alone in the house, because I was sure that he knew more about those men on the ridge than he was telling.

He had walked off directly toward the ridge when he left us by the pond. Directly toward the place where the shots came from a few minutes later. He must have seen the men, and he knew they were doing something besides shooting at targets. And they sure weren't shooting at him.

Paramilitary. I though of what Jasper had said and racked my brain trying to remember what I'd heard about them on TV news programs. There were men hiding in the woods, playing war games with real weapons, pretending to be soldiers, defending whatever they believed in against whatever they thought was evil. But some of them were criminals who stole their weapons from the real army, and they robbed banks and killed people.

And Jasper's beloved Cissy was mixed up with them somehow. She had married one of the men who lived at the old farm, then moved away. Maybe she and her husband didn't want to go along with the terrible war games anymore.

But she came back—with a lot of money and a bruise on her face.

Did she know what was in the box? No, because she wouldn't have forgotten it so easily.

Was she suppose to give it to the heavyset blond man? Or was he there to take it away from her?

Was he looking for me now—to take it away from me?

"Caroline!" Jasper whispered loudly from the stairs.

I jerked around in my chair.

Jasper looked sick. "He's out there, in the backyard."

"Who is?" I whispered.

"That fat man I saw on the ridge."

The man from the depot in Harper's Fork. I got to my feet. My legs felt as if they were made of rubber.

"I saw him through my window," Jasper whispered. "He's in the orchard, about halfway back where the old dead tree is."

I carefully pulled back a corner of the curtain that hung over the kitchen window. I couldn't see anything, but I believed Jasper.

My heart was beating wildly in my throat as I crept across the floor and turned the key in the door lock.

"The front door," Jasper whispered, and I nodded. The living room seemed to be a million miles away as I slipped down the hall, with Jasper right behind me. I was too scared to look out the glass in the door—I just turned the knob on the old-fashioned lock as quietly as I could. Those old locks wouldn't keep anyone out, but at least we'd know someone was coming. Breaking open a door makes a lot of noise.

"Call Gram!" Jasper begged.

"I still don't know the number," I told him, and Jasper's eyes filled with tears.

"Call somebody!" he said. "Call David!"

I nodded and hurried for the phone. The line must be free by now. And if it wasn't, I'd just dial the operator and ask her to get the police. Even if Jasper and I were blamed for having the money, I decided being in trouble with the police was a lot safer than being in trouble with strange men who wore uniforms and hid in the woods.

But as I turned into the kitchen, I heard someone trying the back door and not trying to sneak in, either. The knob rattled and the voice I remembered from the depot called out, "Okay, kids. Open up. We know you're in there."

Jasper shot away from me and scrambled up the stairs. I was tempted to follow him, but there was no telephone extension upstairs, and now I had to tell the operator to send the police to the house.

I lifted the receiver and dialed "0." Nothing happened. The line was dead.

I swallowed against the pulse hammering in my throat.

"Open up!" the man shouted. "This is the police! You don't want to get in trouble, do you, kid?"

For a moment, I was tempted to believe that

he was what he said he was. It would be so easy to let an adult take over, I thought. I wouldn't have to try to be brave anymore. Someone else could make the decisions.

But I was sure that he wasn't a police officer. I rushed up the stairs and straight to Jasper's room. "Did you call Gram?" he asked.

I shook my head. "The telephone line is dead."

"Then what are we going to do?"

I took a deep breath. "We're going to do what Bugman would do right about now. We're going to get out of here."

"Out the window?" Jasper whispered. "Are you crazy? The man is on the porch. If we crawl out on the porch roof, he'll hear us."

Jasper was right. "Then we'll have to wait until he breaks in the door. If he's inside—and we're quiet—he won't hear us climb out."

"But he'll come upstairs looking for us," Jasper said. "We won't have time to get out and my door doesn't have a lock on it."

If we moved a piece of furniture to block the door, we'd make too much noise and the man would hear us. "Let's look in my room," I said.

We tiptoed across the hall. My door didn't have a lock either. And my window was no help—there was no roof outside that window to crawl across. The only thing outside that window was a long drop to the ground underneath—and another man walking toward the front door. I recognized him immediately. He'd been with the men in the woods and now he began pounding on the door. Jasper and I fled to his bedroom.

"Shut the door," I whispered. I gathered up

the small rug that lay on the floor next to Jasper's bed and shoved it against the door. Doors stick on rugs all the time. Maybe Jasper's door would stick on the rug and give us a little more time to make it across the porch roof to the side of the house closest to the woods.

The man at the back door had given up hoping that he could bully me into unlocking the door. He kicked it in. I shoved open Jasper's window and grabbed his arm.

He had the duffel bag again. "Drop it!" I whispered. Who cared about the money anymore? But Jasper was so scared that his fingers had frozen gripping the bag. I shoved him and the bag out the window, and crawled out after him.

We crept across the roof and I strained my eyes in all directions looking for any other crazy soldiers. Their uniforms would be hard to pick out, but as far as I could see, the two men we knew about were the only ones around.

I heard the man who broke open the back door—he didn't make any effort to hide. He thundered through the first floor of the house, yelling for us to come out. After a moment or two, another voice joined his, and I knew he had let the man on the front porch in. They'd be upstairs in another few seconds.

We were on the side of the house now and we'd almost run out of porch roof. "We'll have to get off here," I whispered to Jasper. "Quick, give me your hands."

But Jasper was one jump ahead of me. He slung the duffel bag over his shoulder, knelt on the edge of the roof, and slid over the side, dropping into the snowball bush underneath us.

The men were thudding up the stairs when I dropped off the roof. Jasper and I ran wildly toward the woods and I hoped the rug would block the door long enough for us to cross the hundred feet between Gram's yard and the heavy brush that edged the deep woods stretching east to the ridge and south to the town. We'd go that way, I thought. South.

And then we were in the woods. I grabbed Jasper and we stopped, gasping for breath and listening.

We could hear the men too clearly for them to still be in the house. They knew what we'd done and they were on their way.

Jasper and I panicked. He ran in one direction and I ran in the other. I realized too late that we were separated and I desperately wanted to yell "Drop the bag!" Jasper still had it with him, with the package inside. The men might leave us alone if they had the money. But I was afraid to call out to Jasper for fear the men would hear me.

And then I thought, what if they pick up the box and decide they don't want anyone around who knew they had the money? Jasper and I would be even worse off.

Chapter Eight

NOW I KNOW WHY people say darkness "falls." In the forest, it does. All that hot afternoon I floundered around in the woods collecting cuts and scratches on my arms and legs, and then all of a sudden it was dark and I was in even bigger trouble. I didn't know where Jasper was, I didn't know where those men were, and I had no idea how I was supposed to behave in the woods since I've always loathed camping or anything else connected with dirt, cold water, insects, and meals made up of dried strips of meat and stale crackers.

Jasper, on the other hand, went camping as often as anyone would let him, and in spite of being merely an infant, was reputed to know how to cook over an open fire and stay dry in a storm. Or so the adults in our lives proclaimed when desperately scratching around for something good to say about the kid.

When darkness dropped on me like a curse, I sat down on the nearest log and waited for inspiration—or the sight of a camp fire glimmering between the trees. I didn't get either. If Jasper was busy lighting fires, he was too far away to be of any help to me. I didn't have the slightest idea what to do next.

And I was worried about Gram. What would she think when she got home and we weren't there? And suppose the men were still at the house. Would they threaten her? Or would they realize that she didn't know where we were, either?

The night air was cold. I hugged myself and shivered while I tried to decide what to do. Wandering around in the dark woods didn't seem to be practical, since I didn't know where to go anyway. Back to Gram's? Even if I could find my way, that wasn't much of an idea. The men could find me there. Since Gram's place would be downhill from anywhere on the ridge—and I was surely on the ridge—my safest path seemed to be uphill. Maybe I'd hit a road that would lead to town and to the police. So uphill I went, feeling my way through brush and between trees until it finally occurred to me that I was making enough noise to wake the dead.

"You make enough noise to wake the dead," Jasper whispered out of the darkness behind me. "Don't you know how to walk through the woods without being heard? Bugman—"

"Oh shut up, you little creep!" I cried. "I was afraid something had happened to you." I'd been too scared to put that thought into words even in my head, and here it came popping out my mouth like a toad. Jasper would never let me live it down.

"You were worried about me?" he exclaimed incredulously. "I'm a Boy Scout and a guide and a junior rescue volunteer. The only reason I'm moving around after dark is to catch up with you and stop you from making all that racket. It's dangerous! Now let's make camp for the night."

I gawked through the dark at him, barely making him out. "Make camp? With what? We don't have anything to start a fire with except your Bugman comics and the money."

Jasper's voice was closer, quieter. "We can't have a fire, you dummy. Those men would see it—or smell it. I mean it's time for us to fix ourselves a place to sleep. At first light, we'll move on."

"Move where?" I asked angrily. "Where can we go?"

"We can't go farther up the ridge because the trees thin out there and they'll catch us. And we can't go back to Gram's. So we'll try to get to town by circling through the woods until we come to a back road."

He sounded so sure of himself that I let my muscles relax for the first time in hours and I nearly fell down. "All right," I said begrudgingly, "but I still don't know what you plan to make a camp out of." I hated to admit it to myself, but I was almost glad Jasper was with me.

Jasper pulled me under the sheltering branches of a big fir and dug around in old, dry needles until he scooped out a couple of hollows. "Now do what I do," he said, and I peered through the dark and watched him as he settled down into one of the hollows, curled himself around his duffel bag, and clawed dry fir needles and other stuff over himself. "Never mind the beetles," he said cheerfully. "They don't bite."

I didn't believe that—I lay down in the hollow and tried to warm myself by wrapping my arms around myself and pulling my knees up under my chin. The fir needles were dry under me, but I shook with cold, so after a while I reached out one hand and scraped who-knows-what over me until I'd created an itchy blanket of dry needles and dirt (and beetles).

In books, this is the part where the girl falls asleep in spite of her discomfort and at dawn wakes up refreshed and full of brilliant ideas. That's not what happened. I lay awake all night listening to the forest sounds—quiet rustles and sighs, creaks and thuds. A few times I heard terrifying sounds—wild cries I thought might be birds—or children—being hurt. Or killed. I knew that Jasper was wide awake, too. I could tell because I could hear him scratching his bug bites all night long.

When dawn came, damp and gray and bone-deep cold, the only brilliant idea I had was to spend the rest of my life avoiding my cousin. If he hadn't needed a keeper, maybe my mother would have let me stay home alone those four days and none of this would have happened.

I sat up, brushing unspeakable dried gunk off myself, and sighed. No. Mother would have made me go to Gram's anyway, so one way or another I would have ended up right where I was.

"I have to go to the bathroom," Jasper said from his dugout.

"I'm not stopping you," I responded sourly.

"Well, just don't look," he said as he tottered off into the thicker part of the brush around us, still dragging that darned duffel bag behind him.

I staggered off in the opposite direction, took care of the necessities, and returned to sit under the tree again. In dawn's unflattering light I could see that my shirt was torn, I was absolutely filthy, and I was covered with insect bites which I refused to scratch with my dirty and broken fingernails for fear I'd get blood poisoning. And I was hungry.

When Jasper came back, I asked him if he had anything to eat in his bag. He did. He produced several wads of partially chewed gum preserved in bits of paper (maybe for scientific research) and half a candy bar that looked older than I was. And Cissy's package, of course. He also had three Bugman comics, the ones he couldn't get through the night without. Good grief.

"Let's eat Cissy's cookies," I said, and for once Jasper didn't argue. We ripped off the birthday wrapping paper, opened the box, and divided the cookies between us. Neither one of us lifted the cardboard and checked the money underneath. We knew it was there.

After we finished the cookies, I crumpled up the wrapping paper and was about to throw it out into the bushes when Jasper grabbed it and stuffed it back in his duffel bag. "Don't make it easy for them to track us," he said pompously.

"Oh, for Pete's sake," I complained, but I knew he was right. And I was privately proud of him for being so smart.

The sun was up now, but I wasn't any

warmer. Jasper filled in the hollows we'd used as beds, and together we started walking, keeping high ground on the left because we didn't want to go any farther up on the ridge. We were following what Jasper called a deer trail, but we didn't see any deer. Birds and squirrels watched us as we trudged, and I hoped Jasper still knew what he was doing.

Apparently he did, because after what seemed like days but was probably only an hour or so, we came to a narrow, overgrown road snaking its way through the woods. Jasper put the duffel bag down and sat on the ground next to it. I collapsed beside him.

"We turn to the right here at this intersection?" I asked.

"Ha ha," Jasper said bitterly. "Where else? If we go left, I bet we'll end up on the other side of the ridge, where I saw the old farm."

"This road starts in town?"

Jasper shrugged. "I guess. Near it, anyway. It's probably an old logging road. If we can get back to town where there are lots of people, we'll be okay."

We sat there for a while, letting the sun warm us and maybe dozing a little. I don't remember hearing a thing, but suddenly I was looking at legs and feet—lots of them. The legs and feet were attached to men and one of them was the puffy blond man who wanted Cissy's package.

"Okay, kids," another man said. "The game's over." They all had rifles, not pointing at us exactly, but still threatening

Jasper scooted away from the duffel bag. His glasses hung crazily on his dirty face and I could see from the way he was blinking that he was scared. "Take it," he said.

One of the men bent down and snatched up the bag. "This is it?" he asked, looking directly at me. He had bloodshot brown eyes—I guess he hadn't had much sleep the night before, either.

I nodded.

"You know what's in the box?" the blond man asked sharply.

There was no point in lying. No one would have walked around with that box as long as we had without looking inside.

"Money," I croaked. "But we don't know whose and we don't care. We just want to go home."

The man who spoke to us first said, "Get up." We got up. He gestured up the road to the left. "Get going." We got going.

He seemed to be the leader of the group. Like the others, he wore a camouflage uniform, but he stood a little straighter and his dark hair was shorter. He led the way, Jasper and I followed, and the five other men shuffled along behind. When he asked for our names, we told him. After that no one spoke.

The blond man stayed to one side, as if he didn't exactly belong with the others. We walked a long way up that road until we came to a small clearing where another man sat in a jeep. He jumped out as soon as he saw us, and the leader spoke quietly to him.

At last he turned his attention to us again. "Get in the back," he said. We got in the back of the jeep as fast as we could.

He sat in the driver's seat and dropped the

duffel bag to the floor. The blond man got in next to him and pulled the duffel bag to his lap. The leader glanced at him sharply. The blond man said, "We've had enough screwups." The jeep started and turned up toward the ridge, and if I hadn't been so scared, I would have burst into tears.

Chapter Nine

THE ROUGH TRACK WE traveled over couldn't really be called a road. It was so rocky that there were times I was afraid the jeep would tip over. The woods were thinner here and the brush had gone brown. Once Jasper nudged me and pointed to the left where a huge, jagged rock loomed over us. He leaned toward me and whispered in my ear, "That's Piper's Rock. They're taking us to the old farm."

Great, I thought. Now I get to meet the friendly farmer who scared Jasper out of his wits.

The blond man slung his arm over the back of the driver's seat and turned to look at us. Jasper and I avoided his eyes. After a few seconds he lost interest in us and stared ahead again, but his arm remained over the back of the seat, as if to let us know that he could reach back and grab us any time.

He was wearing a watch and when I saw the

time, I was startled. Seven-fifteen? Was that all? I would have bet anything that the day was half over. Gram must really be frantic, I thought. When she got home and found us gone, she might have believed that we were off somewhere having a good time—until she noticed that the lock on the back door was broken. What must she have thought then? And when we didn't come home all night? The police would be looking for us by now. Would they look up here on the ridge? Or at the farm, where we were being taken?

The jeep rumbled and bounced over the top of the ridge and started down the narrow, twisting trail on the other side. Jasper stared straight ahead through his dirty glasses, but I saw him dig part of his precious collection of lottery tickets from his pocket. He shifted the bits of cardboard from one hand to the other, then dropped one over the side of the jeep. Another time I might have pointed this out to him, but at that moment I couldn't have cared less if Jasper lost every lottery ticket he owned, even the one that didn't have all the stuff scratched off the numbers yet.

The farm. I saw it below us, acres and acres of pasture surrounding a big yellow house and several outbuildings in various stages of collapse. But we didn't go there. Suddenly the jeep veered sharply to the left, and then we were bouncing beside a fence. Ahead of us a small barn leaned toward the ridge. Attached to one side of it, almost out of sight in a tangle of dead vines and weeds, was a sort of shed. The silent driver stopped the jeep there.

"Get out," he said to us.

Jasper and I climbed out of the back of the jeep and the driver shoved us toward the shed.

I thought my heart would stop beating when I ducked my head and scrambled through the door. The shed had no windows and smelled of damp dirt and mice, and I whirled around, unable to stop myself from protesting.

But it was too late. Jasper was shoved in behind me and the door was slammed shut. I heard a wooden bar fall into place across the door, then footsteps. The jeep's engine roared and our captors drove away.

I don't know how long Jasper and I stood there in the near-dark. Finally our situation really hit me.

"We might as well sit down," I said to him. "I have a feeling we're going to be here a long time."

"Right," Jasper said morosely. We eased ourselves down in the dark and I hoped that I wasn't sitting on something that would object.

The shed walls were made of splintery old boards and light seeped in between them. After a while my eyes adjusted and I could see a little of what was in the shed with us. It wasn't much. Some big sacks, filthy and half rotted, were thrown in one corner. A rusty bucket sat in another.

"Bugman has been in worse places," Jasper said.

"If you mention Bugman again, I'll kill you myself," I said. Already the air in the shed was stifling and I dreaded to think what it would be like at noon. Or later. "We've got to think of a way to get out of here, and we don't need ideas that come out of comic books."

"Go ahead and make fun of Bugman," Jasper cried. "Just go ahead. But I learned a lot, reading about him. For one thing, I learned to leave a trail behind me if I was ever captured, so I dropped lottery tickets."

"I saw you drop a ticket on the road," I said, "but I didn't see you drop any others."

"Neither did the men," Jasper said smugly. "Now anyone going along that old road will see them and follow us to this shack."

I pulled my knees up and rested my forehead against them. "Nobody's going to be looking for things like that. And there's garbage all over the world. Who would think you dropped them deliberately?"

"Well, it was better than not doing anything!" Jasper exclaimed.

I couldn't argue with that. In fact, I didn't want to argue at all. It was too hot in that shed, and as the day went on, it got hotter. After a while Jasper and I lay down on the sour-smelling dirt, panting and sweating and sure we were going to die from heat exhaustion.

The sun must have been directly overhead when we heard the jeep coming back. Both of us sat up, waiting for whatever was going to happen and certain we wouldn't like it.

The bar was lifted away from the door and the door swung open, letting in wonderful fresh air—and a girl about my size, carrying two paper bags. I blinked against the dazzle of sunlight.

"Cissy!" Jasper croaked.

I recognized her bruised face. She was still

wearing the red vest just like mine, but hers was clean. Mine was as dirty as my jeans.

I saw someone else, too. A man stood in the doorway behind her, holding a rifle.

"Here's some food and water," Cissy said as she thrust the bags at us. She would have left then, but Jasper grabbed her arm. The man in the doorway stepped inside and raised the rifle —Jasper let go Cissy's arm.

"I wasn't going to hurt you, Cissy!" he protested. "You know I wouldn't hurt you."

They weren't worried that he'd hurt her— they were worried that we were going to try to run off.

But Cissy said, "Sure. I know you wouldn't hurt me. I gotta go now." She started out the door.

"Cissy!" Jasper yelled. "Tell them to let us go. We won't say anything about the box or what was in it. Honest, we won't!"

"We won't!" I echoed. Was Cissy part of this group of crooks or was she held prisoner, too? I couldn't tell. She looked almost as scared as we were.

"Cissy!" Jasper shouted. "Please don't leave us here! We promise not to tell, ever!"

The jeep started up and roared away.

Jasper and I sat down again, back to back. I was glad he couldn't see my face because tears were leaking down my cheeks. I heard Jasper sniffle and knew he was crying, too.

"We'd better eat," I said suddenly, to distract both of us. "Open your bag, Jasper." I wondered when we'd get to eat again. Or if we ever would.

Jasper had a plastic bottle of water and four

apples in his bag. I had four cheese sandwiches in mine. My stomach let me know that no matter how scared I was, this was a good time to eat. We finished off everything except two of the apples and some of the water, and things looked a little brighter.

"Maybe we could break through one of the walls," I suggested. "These boards don't look very strong."

First we took turns kicking the walls of the shed but nothing happened. Next we took turns running at them and thumping our shoulders against the boards. Nothing happened except that we gave ourselves bruises. Then we took turns banging the bucket against the boards until we put more dents in it.

"Maybe we'd better save that bucket," Jasper said.

"What for? It's all rusty."

"We might need it," Jasper said significantly.

"Oh," I said. "Right." There was no nice clean bathroom connected to our little shed. I put the bucket back in its corner and sat down again on the spongy dirt. I was so frightened—and angry. All sorts of ideas of revenge ran through my mind.

Flies had no trouble getting in the shack, and they added to our misery. We covered ourselves with the rotted sacks and made ourselves even hotter, but at least the flies couldn't bite anymore. I tried to remember one other time in my life when I'd been that scared and miserable. I wanted to tell myself that I was going to survive. But I just didn't think I was.

Jasper heard the sound first. "I hear a horse!" he exclaimed, sitting up and throwing nasty sacks in all directions.

Then I heard it, too. We scrambled to the walls, peering through cracks and out into the white-hot afternoon.

"I can't see anyone," I said, changing from one spot to another frantically.

"Wait! I do!" Jasper cried.

I rushed to his side of the shed and stood over him, looking through the same crack. "Yes! Someone's coming along the fence."

Jasper pushed in front of me. "It's David!"

I could have cheered! David was coming! We hammered on the walls of the shed and yelled at the top of our lungs. I paused long enough to peer out again and saw David's horse galloping toward us.

"We're going to get out of here!" I shouted. "It's all over!"

David was there in seconds and had the bar off the door so we could shove it open.

"You followed my lottery tickets, didn't you?" Jasper shouted, dancing around madly in the doorway.

"I saw 'em, sure, but I was going to check this place out anyway." He gaped at me then. "Are you all right?"

"I'm okay," I said, pushing past Jasper and blinking in the bright sun outside the shack. "Dirty and scared, but okay. Let's get out of here."

What gave us the idea we could walk away? We should have known that the paramilitary creeps would watch us. We heard the jeep before we saw it, but before we could react, it careened into sight on the road beside the fence. A man stood up in front, holding a rifle.

"Run!" David shouted.

The man fired when David reached for his horse. The horse reared and ran off, and David staggered back against Jasper, who fell flat on his face.

"Run!" David yelled again, but it was too late. Jasper had his breath knocked out of him and I was paralyzed by the sight of blood on David's arm. The second shot tore chips of wood away from the shed.

I waited to die.

There were three men in the jeep, two I'd never seen before and the tall, dark man I thought of as the leader. The man with the rifle sat down as the leader got out of the back of the jeep.

"You shouldn't be in such a hurry," he said to us with a smile so cold and mean that he was as frightening as the rifle. "We were coming to get you as soon as we decided what to do with you."

He glanced down at David, who was white-faced and very still, holding one hand hard against his wounded arm. "And you should have minded your own business, kid."

Another jeep followed the first one. The leader told Jasper and David to get in that one with the two armed men sitting in it. He directed me to the backseat of his own jeep and sat next to me. We rode toward the farm, and no one said a single word.

I thought about my parents. And Jasper's. If

they didn't already know we were missing, they certainly would before much longer. They would be so worried.

I got Jasper and David into this, I thought, and I have to find a way to get us out of it.

Chapter Ten

THE FARMHOUSE WAS A sprawling, one-story building, and as we approached it from the back, I noticed right away that it had been recently painted. On one side, rows of cornstalks grew head-high, and in the nearest field half a dozen cows dozed in the shade of a clump of trees. It looked like an ordinary farm, the sort you see all over Washington. The difference was what was going on in front of the house.

As the jeeps followed a curve in the track, I saw a big truck parked outside the house—and men carrying long flat boxes from the truck to a hole in the ground beside the garage. The hole must have been the entrance to an underground room, because I saw three men disappear into it, one right after the other. They came out empty-handed, stared at us in the jeeps for a moment, and then hustled right back to the truck and took more of the flat boxes away.

The puffy blond man leaned against a van, watching them. He looked up as the jeep I rode in passed him, then looked away indifferently. I realized then that he didn't care what I saw and neither did the men in the jeep. There was only one reason they wouldn't care—they didn't expect David, Jasper, and me to tell anyone—ever.

The jeeps stopped outside the attached garage. "Get out," the leader said to me, shoving my shoulder a little for emphasis. I got out, stiff and hurting all over. He gestured toward the garage with his gun and I headed to where he pointed—an open door around the corner from the front of the garage.

David and Jasper followed, and the three of us stood in the garage, looking around helplessly. The garage was empty except for a bench against one wall, under a window that had been painted over. The cement floor was oil-stained, but when one of the men told us to sit, we sat. David gasped a little then and tightened his grip on his upper arm. The blood on his sleeve had dried in the heat—maybe he wasn't hurt seriously. But I had to look away. Seeing all that blood made me dizzy.

The door was slammed shut and we heard it locked from the outside.

"Are you going to be all right, David?" I asked quietly, when I thought enough time had passed for the men to have walked away.

"I've sure felt better," he said, and I could see that he was trying to smile.

Jasper fiddled nervously with his glasses. "Caroline, did the men in your jeep say anything?"

"No. Not a word."

"They didn't say anything in our jeep, either. What do you suppose they're going to do?"

I was pretty sure what they *wanted* to do, but I didn't say it aloud, just in case someone was listening and the idea of killing us hadn't occurred to them yet. "I don't know," I told Jasper.

David looked at me strangely and I knew he thought we were in bad trouble.

"Does anyone know you came here to look for us?" Jasper asked David.

"Sure," he said. "Several of us went up on the ridge."

"But does anyone know you crossed over the ridge?" Jasper persisted.

"I told Mike. He didn't think it was such a good idea. Everyone else was sure that you'd come home and surprised a couple of burglars, so they're looking for you all the way to Seattle."

"Burglars!" I said. "Where did they get that idea?"

"Someone went through your grandmother's house and took some of her things. Little stuff, like jewelry and some of her silver."

I pushed my dirty, sweaty hair out of my eyes. "The men must have come back and done that to cover up."

"I didn't believe it," David said. "I walked home with you, remember? When I left, I could hear you two talking inside the house. You didn't sound like you'd just surprised burglars at work."

"The men came later," I said. "One of them,

that fat blond one, was at the wedding. He was looking for me."

David's eyes had been closed wearily until that moment. Now he was staring at me. "What do you mean, looking for you? Is that the guy you told me made a pass at you in the Harper's Fork depot?"

"Yes. That wasn't the truth, though."

"What is the truth, then?" David asked quietly. "You'd better tell me everything."

"Tell him, Caroline," Jasper urged. "Tell him about the box and the money."

When I finished, David sighed. "Boy, are we in a mess," he said softly. "Do you understand what's going on?"

"No," I said. "All I was trying to do was help Cissy, and the next thing I know, I'm kidnapped and locked up in a shed and left to suffocate."

"Those uniforms they wear—the men, I mean. I bet Jasper was right. They're a bunch of crazy survivalists. Paramilitary guys who rob banks to buy weapons."

I remembered vaguely something I'd heard on my little radio while we were on the bus—a news broadcast about a bank robbery in Seattle. I told David. "Do you suppose Cissy had something to do with that? Could she have been moving the money from Seattle to Clayborne for some reason?"

David shrugged and would have said something, but Jasper interrupted. "Cissy wouldn't rob a bank! She wouldn't do something like that."

I stared at him pityingly. "Think about it, Jasper. She had that box of money at the depot, and when I asked her if she was going to a party, she was so nervous she could hardly talk. Of course she wasn't going to a party! She was taking the money back to Clayborne for those rotten paramilitary guys, I bet!"

"Then why did she leave it at the depot!" Jasper challenged.

He had me there. "I don't know," I admitted.

I heard a key in the lock then. The door swung open and I was almost afraid to turn around and look.

It was Cissy again. This time she held a tray with several soda cans on it, and once she was inside the garage, a man shut the door behind her and locked it. She carried the tray carefully and avoided looking directly at us. When she knelt and put the tray on the garage floor, I saw that she was biting her lips. The bruise on her face, the bruise that had been new and purple on the bus, was now fading a little and turning yellow and green. It actually looked worse than ever. She raised one hand to it, as if she felt my curious gaze.

Jasper rose to his knees. "Cissy," he whispered urgently, "what's going to happen to us?"

She shook her head and stood up straight, anxious to leave. "I'm not supposed to talk to you."

"Help us," David said in a low voice.

Her eyes flickered from one of us to the next and stayed at last on Jasper. "I don't know how," she whispered. "They're watching all the time."

"Are you in trouble, too?" I asked suddenly. I concluded from the bruise on her face that she wasn't willing to go along with everything and someone had hurt her to convince her that she'd better cooperate.

"I have to do what they say," she whispered. "Or they'll tell my husband." She touched her bruise carefully. "The most they would let me do is bring you something to drink."

The man outside pushed the door open suddenly. "What's the delay?" he yelled at Cissy.

She hurried toward the door. "They're hungry, Luke," she said. The door was slammed behind her and locked.

I opened three cans and passed one to David. "Can you manage?" I asked. He nodded silently and reached for the can, and I saw that the palm of his hand was caked with dried blood. Once again I had to look away.

Jasper grabbed a can and drank greedily. As thirsty as I was, I had trouble swallowing. David's arm, Cissy's face—these men weren't playing games, no matter how silly people thought they were when they played soldier in the woods.

After we finished the sodas, we felt better. I discovered that the corner of the garage near the big sliding door was cooler than the rest of it. A small draft blew in between the door and the frame there, and so we moved to the corner and leaned against the wall. We could hear men outside talking and laughing, and after a while the big truck started up and drove away. There was more conversation then—I couldn't make it out—and then a car left, or maybe it was the van the blond man had been leaning against. Footsteps passed the garage door and the door to the house slammed. The afternoon was so quiet then that I could hear the hot wind rustling in the cornstalks.

But I was sure we were not alone and unwatched, and so I didn't even try to open the door. Somewhere out there at least one man in a uniform was watching the garage. That much I had learned—they were always watching.

"You said you told Mike you were coming here?" I asked David, picking up our conversation that had been interrupted by Cissy. I didn't like Mike and I had a bad feeling about his knowing where David had gone.

"Well, I didn't say I was coming to the farm," David explained. His voice sounded tired and shaky. I studied him in the filtered light that came through the white-painted window. His face looked so drawn that I was afraid he would faint. Impulsively I reached for his hand.

He took a deep breath and went on. "I just said I was going to look over the ridge. Actually, he told me to keep away from the farm."

That figures, I thought. He knew these men and he wanted them to have a chance to do whatever they were going to do without the interruption of search parties.

He wanted them to be able to unload the boxes from that truck without the county police seeing it. I'd seen boxes like that in a TV movie.

Guns.

I sucked in breath so hard that my lungs hurt.

"What?" Jasper said. "Why are you breathing funny?"

"There were guns in those boxes," I said.

"Sure," Jasper said, uninterested. "Everybody knows that. When Bugman took on the paramilitary, they were buying guns, too, and they came in boxes like that."

David looked at Jasper with something like respect. "I wasn't sure," he said. "But it crossed my mind."

"So," I said, slowly putting things together, "the money Cissy was carrying, the money from that bank robbery..."

"We don't know if that was where she got the money," David said.

"She wouldn't rob a bank!" Jasper protested.

I turned away from him, angry that he wouldn't even listen to criticism of his precious Cissy. Maybe Cissy didn't rob the bank herself, but she knew who did. And she was carrying the money to the men at the old farm so they could pay for the guns.

I was dead certain that I was right.

We had to get away. There wasn't much chance we were going to be rescued, not if most people thought we'd been abducted by burglars who were now on their way to Seattle or some other big city. Of course, Mike knew what had happened to us—because he was part of it. But I wasn't likely to convince either David or Jasper of that, either. They liked him so much that they didn't notice how evasive and sly he was. And maybe I wouldn't have noticed if he hadn't reminded me of that boy who hung around bowling alleys.

I was certain that I was right about him, too. But I didn't want to end up dead because I was right.

Chapter Eleven

NO ONE HAD A watch so we didn't know how much time passed, but it seemed like days. David slumped back against the wall, and his tan looked faded and chalky. He held my hand and sometimes his fingers tightened over mine. Jasper picked at the hole in the knee of his jeans, now so big that I wondered irritably why he didn't rip off the legs and make himself a pair of shorts and be done with it.

"Quit that," I said. "You make me even more nervous."

He ignored me and went on picking. "Why don't they take David to a doctor?" he asked.

I figured that he already knew why and was trying to start another argument, and David had enough trouble without listening to us bicker about whether or not these horrible men would bother spending time and money on someone who probably wasn't going to be around much longer. Instead of answering Jasper, I sighed.

"Doctors have to report gunshot wounds," David said quietly. "And I don't need a doctor. My arm doesn't hurt much anymore."

He was lying. "Look," I said, "why don't you stretch out and try to sleep for a while? You can put your head in my lap."

"I'm all right," David said, but after a while he let himself down carefully and lay on his back with his head in my lap.

"Caroline," he whispered, and I bent to hear him. "I wanted things to be different."

"What do you mean?"

"I like you so much, Caroline. So darned much." His eyelids flickered and then closed and I wasn't sure if he was asleep or unconscious. I looked away from his face so that he could have privacy in that awful, hot garage where there was no real privacy at all. I wanted to hear him tell me again that he liked me. Someday, I thought, when we're safe, we'll talk about how we feel. If we're ever safe again.

"I wonder if Gram let my tarantula out of his jar," Jasper said. He looked up at me anxiously, his eyes red-rimmed behind his dusty glasses.

Yuck. "Probably," I said, trying to cheer him up. I thought it was unlikely that Gram would remember to exercise a tarantula, especially when both her grandchildren had been kidnapped.

"It's not good for him to be shut up so long," Jasper fretted.

"He'll be fine," I said wearily. Jasper was more worried about the tarantula than he was about himself. "I've heard tarantulas are very tough," I told him to make him feel better.

David gasped in his sleep, where his pain had followed him. Jasper and I watched him until he began breathing easily again.

"Caroline," Jasper said, "are we going to die?"

"No," I said sharply. "We're going to get out of this. People are looking for us and sooner or later they'll look here, even if Mike does try to talk them out of it."

"Why would he do that?" Jasper complained. "Why don't you like him?"

"Because he acts like somebody with something to hide, that's why. Anybody would have been scared back there in the woods when those men were shooting, but he wasn't. He talked about them like they were kids fooling around with toy guns. I think he knows them. Maybe he spies for them."

"In Granite Ridge?" Jasper asked incredulously. "Who needs to spy on anything in Granite Ridge? Bugman says that spies hang out where the action is."

I gritted my teeth. Bugman. Well, maybe Mike wasn't exactly a spy, but he could be a member of that gang, living in Granite Ridge and pretending to look for gypsy moths while he watched to see if anyone got suspicious about the old farm on the other side of Piper's Rock. I told all of this to Jasper.

"That's dumb," he said. "Mike knows everything about moths. Those lousy paramilitary guys wouldn't know a moth from a hornet even if they sat on one. He wasn't scared of the guns because he's been in the woods all summer and he's used to them."

I didn't want to argue with him, even though arguing kept his mind off the mess we were in. "Go look at the window. Maybe there's a place you can see out or maybe you can scrape the paint off."

Jasper got up and examined the window. "It's painted on the outside," he said, "but I can see a little through a couple of the scratches."

"Tell me what you see."

"Just part of the driveway."

"Is anyone out there?"

Jasper squinted through a scratch, moved to one side, and peeked through another. "I can't see anybody."

While Jasper watched, I thought. The garage didn't have a door that opened into the house, just the door we came through and the big door that would slide back on overhead tracks when it was opened. That door was probably locked, too, but even if it weren't, opening it would make so much noise that the people in the house would hear us. Maybe, if we were still here after dark . . .

The key turned in the lock and Jasper leaped away from the window. Cissy was back again, this time with sandwiches wrapped in paper towels. She stopped when she saw David lying with his head in my lap.

"How is he?" she asked me.

I shrugged. David didn't open his eyes, but I had a hunch he was awake and listening because his breathing changed.

Cissy came closer and bent down to look at David's face. The man who always guarded her watched her indifferently for a moment, then shut the door.

"Cissy," I whispered quickly, "David's awfully sick. We have to help him."

She touched David's forehead. "He's hot," she said.

"His wound might be getting infected," I babbled. "Can't you do something for us? You helped Jasper once, remember?"

"The men are going to move you to another place," Cissy whispered. "People are looking for you all over the ridge now. They came here last night, but it's just a matter of time before they come back. The men are waiting for someone to bring a cattle truck. They'll take you out in that, with some of the cows."

"When?" I asked.

But she didn't get a chance to answer because the door opened again and a different man came in then, flushed with anger and moving with tight little jerky steps. One of his ears looked twisted and scarred.

"I told you to watch her!" he yelled at Cissy's usual companion as he pushed past him. "You! Cissy! Get away from them!"

Cissy jumped up, scattering sandwiches on the garage floor. The man grabbed her arm and pulled her toward the door. "You don't learn very fast, do you?" he yelled. He shoved Cissy out the door and the other man slammed it shut.

Old Twisted Ear had such a loud voice that we could hear him clearly through the garage door. "I thought I taught you a lesson when you pulled that stupid stunt at Harper's Fork," he yelled at Cissy. "All the trouble we've got now is because of you. The Major didn't want the money or the weapons here because too many people know about it. Now we've got to move both the weapons and those damned kids, too. You do as you're told after this."

"I was only bringing them food, Chuck," Cissy protested.

"Pete said he straightened you out," Chuck went on angrily. "I think he better straighten you out again when he gets here."

Pete. He must mean Peter Black, I thought. Cissy's husband. Then he was the one who hit Cissy and gave her that awful bruise.

"Well?" Chuck shouted. "What have you got to say for yourself now? You want to wait here for Pete or would you rather we shipped you out on the cattle truck with the kids?"

"I want to wait for Pete," Cissy said shakily.

We heard a thud, as if someone fell or was pushed against the door, and then footsteps scuffing away.

David opened his eyes. "I don't think we want a ride on that cattle truck, either," he said.

"You okay?" Jasper asked. "You scared me. I was afraid you were going to die."

David sat up and leaned against the wall. He wasn't feeling any better, I could see that. But at least he wasn't unconscious.

"I don't think we have any choice but to wait for the cattle truck," I said. "I'm sure the garage is being watched."

"Cissy would help us if she could," David said.

"But they aren't going to give her a chance."

I gathered up the sandwiches and offered them to David and Jasper, but both of them shook their heads. I wasn't hungry either.

"What were they talking about outside the door?" Jasper asked.

"I'm not sure," I said, "but it sounded like Cissy didn't do as she was told in Harper's Fork, so someone, probably that fat blond man, brought the truck full of guns here to wait for the money. And someone called the Major—that must be the tall, dark man—was mad about it."

"That's about all I got out of it," David said, "except that this Pete Black is mean to Cissy and she's afraid of all of them."

"I knew she wouldn't do anything bad," Jasper said loyally.

"If we see Cissy again, let's ask her to help us before the cattle truck gets here," I said. "I'm scared of what might happen if they move us."

"The truck must be on its way now," David said, "because the people looking for you two will get here sooner or later and these men can't afford to have searchers poking around when we're locked up in the garage."

"Then we'd better think of something," I said.

"I have to go to the bathroom," Jasper said.

David and I stared at each other and then began to laugh. Leave it to Jasper to interrupt life-and-death plans. It was a relief to be reminded of the ordinary world.

"We don't seem to have any facilities here, Jazz," David said kindly when he quit laughing.

Jasper blushed angrily. "I don't know what's so funny."

"I don't either," I said, wiping tears away from my eyes, "because I have to go, too. I guess Mother Nature doesn't care how much trouble we're in."

"So what are we going to do about this?" Jasper demanded.

I got up and tried to grin as I marched toward the door. "They can't kill me for asking," I said, and I hammered on the door with my fist. "We have to use the bathroom!" I yelled. My voice cracked, showing everybody how scared I was, but I called out again, just in case no one heard me the first time. "Hey, somebody, we have to use the bathroom!"

"Shut up in there!" a man shouted.

I bit my lip and raised my fist once more to pound on the door. "We have to use the bathroom!" I yelled again.

There was a long silence and then I heard someone coming. The key rattled in the lock and the door opened.

Luke stared down at me. "Okay, one at a time," he said, and I gestured to Jasper to go first.

Jasper marched out behind the man, the door was locked again, and David and I looked at each other while seconds ticked by.

"When it's your turn, try to see how many are in the house," David said.

"And I'll watch for Cissy. Maybe I'll get a chance to talk to her."

"Don't risk anything," David cautioned. "They'll be watching her, too."

I nodded. The door was unlocked again and

Jasper hurried in. I filed out, following the man across the driveway and down a short path to the front door of the house. Someone opened it from inside and I stepped into the living room.

Except that it didn't look like a living room. I saw a table and several chairs there, along with a television set, and that was it. Several men were watching a game show on the TV and they stared as I passed. A couple of them played with handguns and leered at me. "Hey, sweet stuff, want to play?" one called out. Luke gestured toward a hallway. "This way. Second door on the left," he told me.

I got a quick glimpse inside a bedroom as I went down the hall. Between two sets of bunk beds, the man called Chuck sat in a chair, holding a gun magazine. He glanced up as I hurried to the bathroom and closed the door.

I looked in the mirror and nearly cried out. My parents wouldn't have recognized me at that moment. I was filthy and my hair was matted and snarled. My chin had been scratched at some time or other—the scratch was red and angry-looking—and my eyes were bloodshot. I was so scared I didn't really care. I took time to splash cold water on my face until it was a little cleaner and then I turned my attention to the bathroom window.

I had a clear view of the ridge, and who should be coming toward the house but Mike Slattery, leading David's horse by the reins. Mike had been gathering specimen boxes again—or pretending to—because half-a-dozen bright orange boxes bobbed and jiggled from strings tied around his neck.

He was still a long way away from the house and I knew he couldn't see me. Would it be worthwhile to try to attract his attention? I didn't have the faith in him that Jasper and David had, so I stepped back from the window.

The man outside the bathroom rapped sharply on the door. "Time's up," he said.

As I walked down the hall, I looked across the small dining room and into the kitchen. Cissy was there, washing dishes at the sink. Curtains were drawn over the window. She didn't know that Mike Slattery was coming and I didn't tell her.

The leader—the Major, probably—was sitting behind his desk now, murmuring into a telephone. He stared as I walked by.

David was standing at the garage door when I returned. I tried to signal with my eyebrows that something interesting was about to happen, but I'm sure he didn't get the message. He stumbled a little as he went out the door and I winced to see him. The door slammed and locked.

"Jasper!" I hissed as I rushed to the window. "Mike Slattery is coming, with David's horse."

Jasper almost beat me to the window. We peered through scratches but couldn't see anything.

But we heard the horse coming a few minutes later. It clopped slowly toward the house and I wondered how far it had run before Mike caught it. And why was he bringing it here?

"What do you want?" a voice called out.

Jasper and I stared at each other. I held my breath while I listened to the horse coming closer and closer. Why didn't Mike say something! What was going on? I peered through a scratch on the window—and there was Mike, in the driveway.

"Is this your horse?" Mike said to the man, as calmly as if this were any ordinary farmhouse. "I found her wandering up there on the ridge."

"I never saw her before," the man said.

Long pause. The horse was standing still now. "Is anyone else here?" Mike asked. "Maybe they know who owns the horse."

"Nobody else is here right now," the man said, but he gestured toward the garage. He was warning Mike that we were close enough to hear him!

"Too bad," Mike said, still speaking in that sly and easy way of his.

The horse stirred restlessly and whinnied. Mike made soothing sounds, then said, "If you're sure you don't know who owns the horse, I'll be on my way. Maybe the folks at the next farm will recognize her."

"Yeah, sure," the man said.

"See you later," Mike said.

Jasper lunged toward the big garage door and I grabbed his arm and jerked him back. "Don't!" I whispered. I pulled him toward the far wall of the garage where there was less chance of anyone hearing us. "The men have guns. There's nothing anyone can do right now. Anyway, I bet Mike knows we're here."

"You're crazy, Caroline!"

I heard the horse walk away and I held on to Jasper until I was sure Mike was gone. The door opened and David came back, looking a little cleaner. He'd washed the blood from his arm—his shirt sleeve dripped water.

He saw me looking at his arm and he touched it gingerly. "It's not as bad as it looks," he said. And then he lowered his voice. "Did you hear Mike?"

"Sure, and I saw him through the bathroom window, too," I said.

David's look was so intense that he scared me. "Did he see you?"

"No."

David sagged with disappointment. "Darn. I heard his voice when I was coming through the living room, but they pushed me back against a wall so he didn't see me."

"He knows we're here," I said. "The other man pointed to the garage when Mike asked him if anyone else was here."

"I didn't see that!" Jasper argued. "And why would he be asking that man who owned the horse? He knows that the horse is David's. He was pretending that he didn't know so he had an excuse to come here. And he doesn't know we're here because you stopped me from telling him."

"There's something funny about him," I began but I stopped. Two pairs of eyes warned me off and I wondered what it would take to convince them that Mike was not all he seemed. I trusted my instinct on this, not their faith in his gypsy moth story.

I couldn't begin to explain why he would come to the farmhouse and say that he didn't know who owned the horse. Or why he would act like he didn't know the men who lived here. Maybe someone was watching the house—the county police, for instance—and Mike wanted to warn the men inside, so he came pretending that he didn't know them and slipped them a message somehow. Maybe. Anyway, I wasn't going to pin my hopes on him. If we were going to get out of this, we'd better come up with an idea all by ourselves.

Chapter Twelve

WE DIDN'T HAVE TIME to think up anything. Without warning, the big garage door slid up with a bang. I gulped in fear and fresh air at the same time. Luke and Chuck stood in the open doorway. "Get up. You're leaving," Luke said.

I hadn't heard the truck until the door opened, but now I did. A heavy engine labored noisily down the rough road that passed in front of the house and then turned in the driveway. I'd seen cattle trucks before—this wasn't one of the really big ones, but it didn't look too comfortable and I wasn't anxious to ride anywhere with a bunch of strange cows, especially since it was likely to be my last ride.

And then the thought struck me that this wasn't a very smart way of smuggling kidnap victims away from a house—the cattle truck looked like a pen on wheels. Anyone could see inside.

But the men were one jump ahead, as usual.

When the truck backed up to the garage and the men let the ramp down, I saw that someone had built a sort of cupboard in the back out of new wood. It wouldn't be big enough to stand up in, but there was room for several people to sit. A shiny new padlock hung from the cupboard's open door.

"Get in," Chuck said, waving his rifle toward me.

"They'll suffocate in there," I heard Cissy cry out from the walk leading to the front porch. She must have run out of the house when the truck came—she was wringing her hands.

The men ignored her. I wobbled up the ramp and crept through the smelly old truck. When I got to the cupboard, I looked back and saw the men shoving David up the ramp. Behind them, Jasper was sliding his hand out of his pocket. A lottery ticket dropped to the driveway.

You're going to get us killed with your Bugman stunts, I thought. But then, what did it matter? We were probably going to get killed no matter what Jasper did. He walked up the ramp, pale and nervous, and joined David and me standing outside the cupboard.

"You can't put them in there!" Cissy cried. She was halfway up the ramp, still wringing her hands.

The Major stepped into view behind her. "I've had all I'm going to take from you," he said angrily.

"You want her moved to the other farm, Major?" Luke asked.

The Major seemed to hesitate for a moment, then he nodded. "Put her in front."

"Pete..." Cissy began.

"Pete does what he's told to do," the Major said. "Maybe he can teach you to do the same."

Cissy watched while the men shoved us into the cupboard, closed and padlocked the little door. I heard Jasper gasp once.

"They drilled air holes for us," David said, but I had seen them already. There were lots of them in the boards in the top of the cupboard and several on each side. I hoped that would be enough—the cupboard was hot already.

I drew my knees up under my chin and hugged my legs, trying to be comfortable. There might be room for all three of us to lie down, but we'd be crowded. If David lay down and rested and Jasper and I sat...

"Look out the holes on the sides," David whispered. "When we get started, try to see if you recognize anything. Maybe we can shove these top boards loose and escape and find our way to someplace we know."

Jasper and I watched from one side and David from the other. I had the silliest thought then. I hadn't had a shower for what seemed like a zillion years—did he notice how awful I smelled?

But then my common sense returned. Someday, I thought, if we're very lucky, David will see me in a dress, clean and fresh, and all this will be like a bad dream. But right then we were about as lucky as the people who bought Jasper's old lottery tickets. And that reminded me of something.

"I saw you drop a lottery ticket," I whispered in Jasper's ear. "Don't you think the men will see it?"

"I hope they're too dumb to notice," he whispered back. "I dropped one in the garage, too. And I left one in the bathroom."

"I didn't see it."

"It's under the sink."

"You really think someone is going to search the house? Someone who will know those lottery tickets belong to you?"

"Mike knows," Jasper whispered.

Oh, great, I thought. If Mike saw them, he'd gather them up, laugh, and never tell anyone. But there was no point in telling Jasper that. If he really thought that Mike was going to rescue us, maybe he wouldn't worry as much as I was worrying. Jasper was only ten, and he'd been scared enough for a whole lifetime. Without thinking, I reached out and brushed dust off his shirt. Poor little kid.

The truck started up and drove a little way over rough ground. I heard the ramp being let down again, and the low, gentle protest of cows. Heavy feet struck the ramp and I could smell the cows then. I couldn't tell how many were driven into the truck, but it seemed to me that there were many big, heavy bodies on the other side of the wood wall of our prison. And many big feet.

The truck started again, lumbered along a bumpy track for a while, and then turned sharp right and roared out on a smooth road, a highway. I saw brush and trees out the ventilation holes on my side of the cupboard, but after a few minutes, David whispered that we were driving through Clayborne.

"Let's yell for help," Jasper suggested.

"Those men have guns," I reminded him.

I saw a few familiar buildings through my ventilation holes, and then brush and trees again. The truck veered sharply to the left not too far from Clayborne—I thought I knew the road they were taking. They were avoiding the highway that passed Harper's Fork and using a smaller road that went east for miles and miles. I didn't know where.

"Poke a lottery ticket out one of the holes, quick!" I told Jasper.

"I've only got a few left!" he protested.

"Maybe someone will see it and know we've turned off the other road!"

Jasper squirmed around until he could reach his pocket, then stuffed one of the lottery tickets through a hole. I kept my fingers crossed that it would fall where it could be seen.

Sometimes we passed houses and farms, but I didn't recognize anything now. The truck engine began making strange noises but, to our disappointment, it kept running. "Do you know where we are?" I asked David.

"We're heading east toward the foothills," David said.

A horrid thought brought my heart to my throat. "Do you think they're taking us over the pass to Eastern Washington? You can drive for miles there without seeing people. Will anyone look for us on the other side of the mountains?"

"I hope so." David sounded so sick. And worried.

The truck labored up a long, steep hill, and near the top the engine coughed and stopped. We heard the men swearing as they climbed out, and David squeezed my hand hard. "Maybe they can't start it again."

The men had a long conversation we couldn't hear well enough to understand, and then footsteps faded away.

"They're leaving us!" Jasper cried.

We didn't waste any time. Jasper and I crouched with our backs against the top of the cupboard and when David counted to three, we tried to straighten up to force the boards loose. Twice we tried, three times, and then, when I was ready to quit, we shoved at it once more, and with a screech, the nails pulled out of the wood.

The cows reared around, mooing and kicking out, and we had to wait until they settled down before we dared push the loose boards all the way off. I got out first, blinded by the light, and I crouched beside the large, muddy hooves of a cow that watched me suspiciously.

"All clear?" David whispered.

"I think so." I blinked against the light that streamed in the truck.

Jasper helped David out and the cows complained again.

"Is anyone outside?" David asked. I tried to see around the cows and out through the slats in the truck, but they wouldn't stand still long enough for me to get a good view of anything.

"Let's just run for it," Jasper said, and he pushed his way past the nervous cows.

Someone stuck the barrel of a rifle through the slats and pointed it at Jasper. I thought my heart would stop. "That was a lot of work on a hot day, kids," we heard Luke say with a laugh. "Now get back in the box."

We obeyed. We heard footsteps, and shortly after that the truck started up with a roar—we were on our way again. After a while Jasper slept, sagging over on David's legs. The air in the box was better now, since the top was off. I leaned my head against the wood and I must have slept, too, because the next thing I knew, the truck had stopped, the cows were stirring restlessly, and I heard voices.

The Major was outside. The truck doors opened and I heard Luke, Chuck, and Cissy speaking softly to him. Where had the Major come from? Had he been following in a car? Why did we think we could escape? It was crazy.

A strange voice said, "What are you planning to do with them?" and I didn't know if he meant the cows or us.

"Run 'em out to the far pasture—there's a barn there and a good creek," another strange voice suggested.

They were deciding the fate of the cows, I realized. Jasper stirred and woke up, clearing his throat with dry coughs.

"Where are we?" he asked.

"At the other farm, I guess."

David coughed, too, and struggled to sit up. "What's happening?"

"Lie back down," I told him. "We've arrived, but I don't think they're going to let us out very soon. They're finding a place for the cows."

The truck started up again and groaned as it labored up a hill, over the worst road yet—or maybe we were sore from all those hours riding on bare wood. After a few minutes the truck turned right, then stopped for a moment while someone got out of the cab, did something, and then got back in again. The truck backed up over rough ground and stopped. Doors slammed and the ramp was let down for the cows, who wasted no time in getting out. A few minutes later, Luke yelled at us to get out.

I squinted against late afternoon sunlight. David sat up with difficulty and more or less rolled out of the cupboard. No one offered to help him, although there were two men standing there watching. Jasper followed stiffly. My legs were asleep and I felt as if needles were being jabbed in them when I stood up. Jasper grabbed my arm when I nearly fell. The two men only watched.

David was tottering down the ramp, clutching his arm again. Jasper and I followed, and I know I was leaning hard on my cousin, but I'd have fallen if he hadn't been there.

I was tired and dirty and half sick, but I was still struck by the peaceful beauty of the scene before us. We were standing on the edge of what seemed to be endless pasture, with grass that grew hip-high. The cows were wading through it in a line, heading toward a lower section where trees lifted branches against the late afternoon sky. The creek must be there, and I wanted to run after the cows and plunge into the cool water, drinking and washing and splashing—and forgetting.

And there was a lot to try to forget. Too much. The men were there, and poor Cissy, who looked like she had spent these last hours crying.

"What are you going to do with us?" David

asked suddenly. I wished he hadn't said it aloud. We knew were in trouble, and I really didn't want to know what would happen next.

"Get in the truck," one man said. "We're taking you to the house."

A house? With a bathroom and soap and water? It's weird how little things like that suddenly seemed so important—more important even than the threat that hung over us. I felt grateful that we were going to have a chance to be inside a house, and I hated myself for feeling grateful to these rotten men. But a house meant civilization and civilization might mean freedom.

They let us ride in the back of the truck where the cows had been kept instead of in the cupboard, and we stood up, as much for the opportunity to stretch our legs as to avoid the dirty floor. The trip back to the house didn't take long enough—I watched the pasture disappear behind a line of trees and I actually wished that someday, someway, I could come back to that place and walk down to the creek. When I caught myself thinking that, I decided that I must be going crazy.

But David said "That was a pretty place," and Jasper said, "Yeah," so I wasn't alone. All three of us were crazy.

The truck stopped and the men put the ramp down for us. We walked out and looked up at the back of an old farmhouse, where thick vines grew over peeling walls and almost obscured the small, narrow windows. The men guided us up the back steps and into an old-fashioned kitchen. Two young women worked there, and they avoided our eyes when we looked at them. Both of them smiled familiarly at the men, though, and the taller woman said, "Hey, fellas, we missed you."

Cissy was following us, and when she saw the two women, she said, "Hello, Lucy! Sharon!"

The women nodded to her but not in an especially friendly way and I could see that Cissy's feelings were hurt. She would have stayed in the kitchen with them, though, except when she stopped, one of the men shoved her behind us. "Keep going," he said roughly.

They took us upstairs to the attic and shut us in a room with a low, sloping roof, one window which fortunately opened so we could have fresh air, and an assortment of old furniture. There were a couple of broken-down beds, so Cissy and I insisted that David lie down on one of them and he didn't argue. His arm looked strange now, swollen so big that his shirt sleeve was too tight on it. Cissy examined his arm for a moment, then stuck her finger in the jagged hole the bullet had torn in his shirt and ripped the sleeve clear to the cuff.

"That feels better," David mumbled. "Thanks."

Cissy worked on the sleeve a little longer until she succeeded in tearing it off at the shoulder. I nearly gagged when I saw David's wound. It had scabbed over and looked more like a huge ragged cut than a bullet hole. The flesh around the wound was red and shiny and his arm was swollen clear to his fingers.

Cissy looked sharply at me. I blinked. David was really sick and we had to get help for him.

Cissy crossed to the attic door and tried the

knob. It was locked, of course. She knocked on the door, and when no one responded, she hammered on it.

Someone downstairs yelled "Knock it off!" but Cissy kept on hammering, and finally we heard footsteps climbing the stairs.

They let Cissy out—I listened to her feet going down the stairs and strained to hear her voice but heard nothing at all after a downstairs door slammed shut.

There was a small bathroom off the attic room and Jasper came out of it, looking relieved and a little cleaner. He had washed his face and hands and slicked back his hair with water, but his glasses were as dirty as ever. Maybe he didn't notice.

"You want a drink of water, David?" I asked. When he nodded, I went into the bathroom. A cracked cup sat on a shelf over the sink. I washed it with soap and rinsed it over and over with water that trickled in a thin stream from an old faucet. There was no window in the bathroom—there was nothing at all except the sink and the john. Not even a mirror on the dirty walls. I brought the cup back to David and he drank half the water, then pushed my hand away.

"I've let you down," he whispered. "I should be taking care of you and Jazz. Caroline, if we get out of this... Oh, Caroline! I'm so darned sick. Kiss me once, please, and tell me you aren't mad at me."

"Of course I'm not mad at you," I said. My eyes filled with tears as I bent over him. "Can't you tell how much I like you? Don't worry anymore. Just get well, David."

I kissed him gently on his feverish lips and held him in my arms until he slept again, then I moved to an old chair against the wall nearest the window and waited with Jasper. I hated that attic. It smelled of old dust and fear, and once I was certain I heard something small and horrid scuttling around under the floorboards.

Jasper discovered that his chair creaked when he rocked it back and forth, so he creaked and I gritted my teeth.

"Where do you suppose Cissy is?" he asked. *Creak. Creak.*

"Downstairs," I said. "Maybe they're not mad at her anymore and will let her alone now. And sit still! You'll wake David." I tried not to remember that Cissy had gone looking for help for David. Apparently she wasn't going to get it.

David slept deeply, breathing in a quick, shallow way. After what seemed like hours, Cissy was let back into the room. She carried strips of old towels and a bottle of alcohol.

"The women in the kitchen gave me these," she said. "It's not much and the alcohol will hurt him, but they didn't have anything else. They won't call a doctor for him."

"He's sleeping now," I said. "Maybe you can fix his arm and he won't wake up."

"He'll wake up," Cissy said unhappily.

David did, with a hoarse cry, when Cissy poured the alcohol on his arm. But he never made another sound while she bandaged it. When she was done, he turned over with his face to the wall and muttered "Thanks."

Cissy and I were both close to crying. Jasper looked as if he was sick to his stomach.

"What's going to happen to us?" I asked. "Did they tell you?"

"They won't talk to me at all," Cissy said. "They don't trust me anymore."

"Because you tried to help us?"

"That. And the other thing. What I did at Harper's Fork."

"But what did you do?" Jasper asked. "What happened?"

Cissy bit her lip again, then shrugged. "I guess it doesn't matter if I tell you," she said. "I was supposed to wait there for Whitey. He brought a shipment from down south and the Major didn't want it delivered at the Clayborne farm because they were planning on leaving there soon anyway. He wanted it delivered at another place they have a couple miles outside Harper's Fork. I was supposed to give the box to Whitey in the Harper's Fork depot, then get back on the bus and go to Granite Ridge, as if I were on my way to the Hooper girl's wedding. No one would think anything strange about that. But I'd never met Whitey and I didn't see anyone in the depot who looked like Pete said he did, and then, well, I heard the bus to Seattle being announced. I was really scared, so I left the box in the place where I was supposed to meet Whitey and bought a ticket and got on the Seattle bus. When my husband found out what I did, he called someone to come and get me. They took me to Clayborne and made me wait with Whitey until the money was found. I don't know what they would have done to me if they hadn't found it."

Jasper looked at me triumphantly—his

adored Cissy was innocent of everything in his eyes. But something was still bothering me.

"Where did the money come from?" I asked.

"My husband got it," Cissy said vaguely.

"He robbed a bank, didn't he?" I asked.

Cissy sucked in her breath. But she wouldn't answer me. She didn't need to. I was sure that was where the money came from, and her husband was afraid he'd be caught if he took the money to Whitey, so he sent poor dumb Cissy to do the rest of the dirty work.

"Your husband is one of them, isn't he?" I asked. "He's one of those survivalists—those paramilitary guys."

"They're going to save the country from Communist infiltrators," Cissy recited like an obedient little kid. She sounded like she'd been brainwashed.

"They're trying to overthrow our government," Jasper said sternly. "Bugman fought them all over the place and got rid of them."

"It looks like he missed a few," I said crossly.

Jasper sagged in his chair, picking a loose thread on his shirt. "Well, it was only a comic book."

"I wish we were living in one of your comic books," I said. "Then we could be sure everything was going to turn out all right."

"The men will probably take you somewhere and let you go after they're sure no one is going to find out about the shipment and the other farms," Cissy said.

I wanted to believe that and I was sure she did, too. But there was a big hole in that idea. We could tell about this farm. Even though we didn't know exactly where we were, we could still describe it and maybe someone would recognize it. No one was going to let us go.

Our discussion came to a quick end when someone unlocked the door and yelled for Cissy. She left and Jasper sighed. David seemed to be asleep again. I looked out the window and watched the sky turn from light blue to deep blue. I turned on the room's single light bulb.

My parents were probably at Gram's now, I thought. Were they scared? Did anyone have any idea what had happened to us? Was there no way we could get out of this?

I leaned on the windowsill and looked down. The ground was a long way away. And directly below me, a man sat in a chair tilted back against the house. In the light from the window behind him, I could see the rifle across his knees.

Chapter Thirteen

"IF YOU WANT SOMETHING to eat, come downstairs."

I snapped awake and sat up straight in my chair. Chuck, the man with the twisted ear, startled me—I hadn't heard the door open and I sure didn't like discovering that I slept so hard someone could sneak up on me.

David lay on the bed facing the wall, and he didn't respond so I knew he was still asleep—or unconscious. Jasper, however, got to his feet stiffly and looked at me.

"Should we eat, Caroline?"

I was hungry, but I wasn't sure if we should leave David alone. I bent over him and called his name—I thought I saw his eyelids twitch, as if he heard me from someplace far away and didn't have the energy to answer. There was nothing I could do for him. Nothing!

"He's awfully sick," I said to Chuck.

"You want to eat or not?" he asked sharply. "Make up your mind."

Jasper edged cautiously toward the door and I decided then that we'd better eat—what good would it do for all three of us to be sick? And maybe they'd let me bring something back to the room for David, just in case he woke up later and felt hungry.

Chuck locked the door behind us and followed us down the uncarpeted steps to the first floor. He reached over my shoulder and gave Jasper a shove toward the right. "Go in the kitchen," he said. "Hurry up."

Jasper blundered through a door and I saw Cissy inside, looking up at us from the stove where she was cooking something in a frying pan. It smelled like canned hash, and my mouth watered.

"Sit," Chuck said, and we sat at the kitchen table. He slammed out the back door then, and through the glass pane in the top of the door I saw him wave to someone and then disappear, as if he'd sat down suddenly on the top step.

Jasper and I sat close together on one side of an old table and looked hopefully at Cissy. The women were gone, but they'd left stacks of dirty dishes and pans behind and I wondered if Cissy was supposed to clean up after everyone.

"It's just leftovers," she said, lifting the pan off the stove and scraping the contents into a bowl. "There's no milk. Sorry. But you can have pop if you want. And there are some biscuits left."

She set the bowl on the table and shoved it toward me. I spooned hash onto my plate and passed the bowl to Jasper. "Take all the rest," I told him. He scraped the bowl clean. Cissy opened pop cans for us and put out a plate of cold biscuits and a container of margarine. As meals go, it wasn't much, but I would have eaten cardboard smeared with paste at that point.

"Can I bring a couple of biscuits up to David?" I asked.

"Sure. How's he feeling now?" Cissy asked. She looked back over her shoulder as she ran water into the sink and I was sure she actually cared. Immediately I wondered how I could turn this to our advantage.

"He needs a doctor. I'm not sure if he's sleeping or unconscious. Can't you do anything?"

Cissy's back was turned to me at that moment and I saw it stiffen. She dumped detergent in the water and slid a couple of dirty plates into the sink. Then suddenly she turned, glanced at the window, and whispered, "They're moving you again."

I stopped chewing. How many times were we going to be carted from one place to another before whatever was going to happen actually happened? "Where?" I asked. "Why?"

Once more Cissy looked at the dirty glass panel in the door. "They're taking you to a cabin a couple of miles off the highway that goes over the pass. Then they're going to try to trade you for three of their friends who were put in prison last year for killing a bank guard."

I swallowed hard. Did this mean we were going to live? I exchanged a quick glance with Jasper, then said, "Are they going to call a doctor for David?"

Cissy shrugged, then shook her head. "I don't think so. They wouldn't want to take a chance on getting caught. They're already wanted by the police."

A knot in the pit of my stomach tightened. "He's got to see a doctor."

"Maybe it will all be over in a couple of days," Cissy said. "He can make it until then." But we all knew that might not be true.

"What will happen to you?" Jasper asked. He poked at his glasses and scowled.

"I guess I'll go with the others and meet Pete in Idaho."

"Aren't they going to use this farm now either?" I asked.

Cissy shook her head. "It's getting too dangerous."

Jasper cleared his throat. "Why don't you ask them if you can stay at that cabin with us?"

But Cissy only shook her head again.

I ate another biscuit while I thought. The paramilitary army seemed to be on the run. The first farm was already abandoned. Cissy had mentioned another place near Harper's Fork, and they must have closed it now, too. And they were running away from this farm. Something must have gone wrong with their plans. I had a hunch people were looking for us—and getting close.

"I hope we don't have to go in that cattle truck again," I said.

"There's no place for cows at the cabin," Cissy said. "They'll take you in a car."

"Who? The Major?"

Cissy turned to look at me again. "Oh, no," she said and she seemed astonished. "He's going to Idaho. Two or three of the men will take you up to the cabin."

"When are we leaving?"

"Tomorrow morning. Early." Cissy washed and rinsed plates mechanically, like a wind-up doll.

"Can't you help us get away tonight?" I asked. "After they're all asleep, you could let us out."

"They'd kill me," Cissy said simply.

"They might kill *us* if they can't trade us," Jasper said in a rough, scared voice.

Cissy started to shake her head, then stopped. I saw her bend over the sink as if something hurt her. She wasn't washing plates anymore—she held her hands in the water, bending over them and breathing in shallow little gasps.

"This place is miles from the nearest town. The people who own it won't help you—they're a part of the army. Where could you go? They'd catch you before you got very far away and everything would be even worse."

"When they're asleep," I whispered, "Let us out and get me keys to a car. I'll drive David and Jasper away from here."

Cissy shook her head. "There will be someone watching."

Jasper said loudly, suddenly, "Can I have some more pop?"

I shot a quick glance at him—he was looking at the door. I could see the back of a man's head through the window. He turned, looked inside, and opened the door.

"Time's up," he said, fingering his twisted ear as if it hurt him. "Go back upstairs."

Jasper and I rose immediately. I closed my hand over two of the biscuits, not certain if he'd make me put them down if he saw them. But he didn't seem to notice, and so I carried them upstairs, wondering if David would be awake to eat them.

He wasn't. The man shoved us inside, seeming to take pleasure in pushing Jasper against me as I walked through the door. Mean, I thought. They're mean people who like doing the things they do. I wished there were a Bugman to catch and punish them.

I knelt by David's bed as the man slammed shut the door and locked it. David's face was flushed and hot and his lips were cracked. I kissed his cheek and whispered his name. He didn't respond, so I put the biscuits down on the windowsill and sat in the chair.

"When David wakes up," Jasper said, "I'm going to tell him what you did. Guys don't like to be kissed all the time and I'll bet your folks wouldn't like you kissing him, and neither would mine—or Grandma, either." He looked like he was ready to bawl.

"Oh just go to sleep," I cried.

"I don't have to do anything you say, Caroline!" he retorted.

"So don't, then," I said wearily. "I'm going to turn out the light now."

He turned a startled, frightened face toward me. "No! I don't want to be in the dark, Caroline."

As a matter of fact, neither did I. The light stayed on.

I don't know how much time passed. Occasionally I could hear people moving around downstairs, and once in a while a door slammed. Two or three cars left—I looked out the window when I heard their engines start and I saw headlights sweep around the house and disappear. I thought first that the Major had left, but later on I saw him outside, standing in the light from the window and looking out over the farm. I leaned on the windowsill and thought about calling down to him, begging him to let us go. But I knew it wouldn't do any good, so I sat back down again, and later, when I looked out, he wasn't there anymore. It was going to be a long night for everyone.

The sounds in the house stopped finally, but outside I could still hear occasional footsteps. Cissy was right—someone was awake and watching.

Jasper had fallen asleep, curled up in a tight, nervous little knot on the middle of the mattress, and I yawned so widely that my jaw made a funny, cracking sound. I reached out to close the window. The night air was cold.

And I stopped with my hand in midair. I heard something outside our door. Not a footstep—no, something different. The rustle of clothing, perhaps, or the scrape of one shoe against another. I stared at the door until my eyes hurt.

A piece of paper eased under the door, a small piece of paper with something on it that reflected light. I got out of the chair, holding my breath, and crept across the floor.

A key lay on the paper. I bent to pick it up, scared that whoever was outside would pull it back if I didn't hurry, or if I hurried too much. My fingers seemed numb and clumsy—I nearly fumbled and dropped the key.

"Cissy?" I whispered.

There was no answer. I didn't hear footsteps going away, but I somehow knew that she wasn't outside the door anymore.

I crept back to my chair, shaky and scared, and sat down to look at the paper and the key. It was an ignition key to a car, and the piece of paper had one word scribbled on it—"Green."

It was the ignition key to a green car or green truck. Cissy had risked a lot to get it to me, and now I wasn't sure what I was going to do with it.

Had she unlocked the door, too? I got up again and tiptoed across the room to try the knob. Locked. Maybe she couldn't get the key to the room. How was I supposed to use the car key if I couldn't get out of the room? Did she think I was going to try to get out the window? Was it possible?

I went back to the window. The light downstairs was still on, and I could see clearly that I was so high up I'd break at least one leg if I jumped. There was nothing I could use to climb down on, no trellis or drainpipe. Nothing at all, just a sheer drop to the hard ground—or the lap of the man who sat in the chair there, tilted back against the house.

And even if I could have climbed down safely, how could I have managed to get David out of the house? I doubted if Jasper and I together could lift him. There was no way we could lower him out of a window.

I shut the window and sat back in the chair. Finally I slipped the key in my pocket, along with the scrap of paper. I didn't know yet how I was going to manage to use the key, but Cissy must have had something in mind. I'd just have to wait until morning and see what opportunity presented itself.

And no matter what happens, I promised myself, I won't give in to being tired or scared. I wasn't sure that Cissy was brave enough to come through for us. I wasn't even sure that she understood that there was nothing good about this secret army of bank robbers and murderers.

And David was too sick to help.

So it's you and me, Bugman, I thought, looking over at my sleeping cousin. Who'd have thought we would ever get together on anything?

Chapter Fourteen

I STRUGGLED THROUGH a peculiar dream while I slept sitting up in the rickety chair.

I dreamed that David and I went to my high school prom together. The dress I wore was the one I'd seen in a department store window the month before—the dress Mom said was too old for me. David wore a dinner jacket and he looked wonderful. Whenever he glanced down at me through his long lashes I could feel a dream blush spreading over my dream face.

But while we were dancing I saw the men from that stupid army come in. They stood by the doorway, watching the dancers—looking for me.

In my dream I tried to tell David what was happening but he couldn't hear me. He smiled and looked around innocently, never realizing the danger we were in.

I panicked and tried to lead him off the dance floor, but my arms were too weak and heavy. My legs wouldn't move. I tried to scream but I had no voice. I was helpless.

And David kept smiling and smiling. He didn't see the men coming toward us. Then I saw his arm. Blood dripped quickly and steadily from an awful wound near his shoulder.

Help us, I pleaded silently to the other dancers.

And I woke up with a start. The helpless feeling from the dream still lingered, and for a moment I had to hold both hands over my mouth to keep from crying.

Scritch scritch scritch.

Jasper was awake, sitting on the edge of his bed and playing around with one of his lottery tickets. I watched him for a moment, then asked him what he was doing.

He didn't look up. "I'm scratching off all the black stuff except for what's right over the number."

"Is that the ticket you found that still has one square covered over?"

He nodded.

"Why don't you scratch everything off it and see what the number is? Maybe you won something." If he discovered he was a winner, I thought, he'd be so excited that he'd forget to be scared for a while.

Jasper looked up at me with a pained expression. "A lottery ticket with a number that isn't uncovered is worth five of the other tickets. I'll need it like this if I'm going to have a chance of keeping the tarantula for another week. I used most of my tickets trying to rescue us and I'm sure not going to ask those crazy men if they have any old tickets. And I'm not going to go through their garbage, either." He heaved a big sigh and went back to his work.

That goes to show how different our minds were. I dreamed about going to a dance with David. Jasper worried about getting the tarantula for another week. I thought how funny it was that the small things suddenly become the most important when you're afraid you'll never get to do them again.

David stirred restlessly and muttered my name. I got up and stood by his bed for a few moments, but he slipped back into deep sleep again, so I went back to my chair.

"David is in bad shape, isn't he?" Jasper asked without looking up.

"Maybe not," I said evasively.

"But probably yes," Jasper argued. He'd stopped scratching the ticket but he still didn't look up. "Maybe David will die before those men can exchange us for their friends," he said.

"Don't be silly."

He looked up then, peering at me through his dirty, crooked glasses. "What are we going to do, Caroline?"

I put one finger over my lips to warn him to be silent, then I pulled the key out of my pocket. Jasper's eyebrows shot up. He scrambled off the bed and across the room. "Is it the door key? Where did you get it?"

I shook my head. "It's a car key. And it came with this." I unfolded the scrap of paper and showed him the word "Green."

"It must mean a green car," Jasper whispered. "Did Cissy give you the key?"

I explained about the key being shoved under the door.

"But how are we going to get out of the room?" he asked.

"I don't know yet. Maybe Cissy has some ideas. We have to wait and see."

"I told you how nice she is," Jasper whispered. "I told you."

"Yeah. I know. Just like Princess Sting." I brushed his hair back from his face and straightened his glasses, the way I'd seen his mother do a hundred times.

Filled with hope now, I tucked the key and the bit of paper back in my pocket. If I didn't think too far ahead, anything seemed possible. Sitting there, I could fantasize about rushing out the next time the door was opened, finding the green car—or maybe truck—and leaping in.

But what about David? He might not be able to do all that running and leaping, and Jasper and I couldn't leave him behind. Even in the short time it would take us to get help (I refused to consider anything other than a very short time), these horrible men could do something awful to David.

Something will come up, I promised myself. Cissy wouldn't have risked giving me the key if there were no way I could use it. But I wished she'd given me a hint of how we were going to pull this off.

"Caroline," Jasper whispered, "do you think Gram told our folks?"

"Of course she did."

"Do you think they're in Granite Ridge already?"

I nodded, wishing he hadn't reminded me. I knew our parents would be half crazy with worry now. Thinking about their fears scared me all over again. What if there was no way to use the key? What if we *died* here?

Jasper sat up very straight. He was working hard to keep his lower lip from trembling.

I slipped out of my chair and sat on the floor next to him. I put my arms around his stiff little shoulders and whispered, "Jasper, don't get mad but I think I'm going to cry."

He patted my knee with a grubby hand. "Go ahead," he said, choking on his own tears. "I'll never tell."

After a while Jasper was all cried out and he crept back to bed. I sat in my chair, sleeping and waking and sleeping again. Somehow the night passed and dawn came.

David woke. I saw him struggling to sit up and I hurried to help him.

"Are you feeling better?" I asked.

"Sure," he croaked. He sagged against me for a moment, then straightened up. "Sure, I feel a lot better."

But in the weak yellow glow of the single light bulb hanging over us, I saw the black circles under his eyes. And I could feel the heat radiating from his feverish body.

Somehow we had to get out of there. David couldn't wait while these crazy men tried to negotiate the release of their friends. There had to be a way I could use that key.

Chapter Fifteen

NOT LONG AFTER THE sun rose, Chuck came for us. He didn't show any sympathy for David. Instead he yelled at him for taking a long time to struggle out of bed.

"Get downstairs!" he shouted at us over and over, and even though we hurried as fast as we could, he shoved Jasper and me so hard I was sure we'd both fall down the stairs.

In the kitchen, the two women I'd seen before handed each of us bread and a cup of coffee. They didn't speak—in fact, they barely looked at us. While we were sitting at the table eating our small breakfast, both women left by the back door. Through the kitchen window I saw them walking toward one of the outbuildings. A heavyset man in jeans and an old shirt went by the window next, and he carried a bucket in each hand. These, then, had to be the farmers who made the horrible army welcome on their land—they were as scary as the Major and his men.

David chewed for a long time on one bite of bread and finally washed it down with coffee. Jasper ate quickly, and every time I looked at him, he was looking at me.

Chuck leaned against the wall, slurping up coffee and watching out the window. After a while he straightened up and said, "That's enough. Let's get going."

He gestured toward the door that led to the hall, so we three filed through and went into the living room. The Major was there, murmuring on the telephone again, and another man was loading papers into boxes. The major hung up when he saw us.

"We're taking you to another place," he said. "If everybody does what he's told, you'll be home in a couple of days."

A couple of days! I hardly dared hope that this would all be over with in a couple of days. We could stand anything until then...

David. I looked at him quickly and he met my glance, grinning. But his face was ashen and he cradled his injured arm cautiously. David couldn't wait for two more days.

"David needs a doctor," I began.

The Major moved his gaze toward me and I looked into his flat, pale brown eyes, and I knew that he didn't care what David needed.

"Put them in the camper," he said to Chuck.

We walked ahead of him while he alternately poked us with his rifle and shoved us with the heel of his free hand. David gasped once and I turned my head sharply to see him bent protectively over his arm and blinking tears away.

We marched through the kitchen and out to

the back porch. Three men in uniform squatted beside the driveway, talking softly to each other. Cissy leaned against the hood of an old green truck, and when she saw me looking at her, she moved away. Of course! The green truck! I had the key to it in my pocket. When Cissy saw me nod, she pretended to lose all interest in us and sat down on the bottom step of the porch.

But how was I supposed to use the key? There were three men there, as well as Chuck. They weren't about to let me stroll over, open the truck door, and start it.

The Major came out on the porch, followed by a man carrying cardboard boxes. "Here, Jim!" he called out to another man. "Grab one of these boxes and help Andy load them in the truck."

Oh, no! They were going to use the truck. I looked at Cissy from the corner of my eye—she was biting her lips again.

Chuck poked and prodded us toward the camper that sat beside a dirty yellow car on the other side of the driveway, almost out of sight of the porch. While he banged his fist on the stuck door of the camper, one of the other men got into the cab, jingling a set of keys. He was the one guarding us when Mike Slattery showed up with David's horse.

Chuck swore and yelled at the man in the cab. "Hey! Did you lock this door? I thought I told you not to lock it."

"It ain't locked," the other man said, laughing. "If you need help, say so."

Chuck swore again and yanked on the camper door. I had a hunch it really was locked, but he had lost his temper by then and was too stubborn to do the sensible thing and ask the other man for the keys.

And the other man was now having trouble of his own. The starter growled and growled, but the engine wouldn't catch. From where I stood, at the corner of the house halfway between the camper and the porch, I could see Cissy watching intently. The two other men stood up and wandered toward the camper, fascinated by the racket Chuck was raising.

The men helping the Major load boxes into the back of the truck let down the tailgate and turned to watch the commotion. I saw the Major sling a box on the truck, then turn and start toward us. The men followed but they were grinning. I began to suspect that they didn't like Chuck any better than I did.

The camper's starter motor was beginning to sound rundown and tired out. One of the men lifted the hood and all the other men except for Chuck joined him and stared down at the engine. Chuck was now kicking at the camper door.

I saw Cissy walking up the steps to the back door. She paused when she saw me looking at her, then made a quick gesture toward the truck. Now was the time.

"Let's go!" I whispered to Jasper.

I grabbed David around his waist and Jasper took his good arm. "Get to the truck. I've got a key," I told David.

He wasted precious seconds staring at me.

"Run!" I urged, pushing as hard as I dared. "David, run!"

It was wild. It was so wild that even while I

was doing it, I couldn't believe I had that much courage. Jasper and I pushed David toward the truck, not taking time to look back to see if anyone had noticed. Of course they noticed! But I didn't dare check them out because I knew my courage would evaporate if I saw anyone running after us.

I saw that the truck's tailgate was still down. "Get David in the back of the truck!" I screamed at Jasper, and I leaped toward the driver's door.

"Come back here!" Chuck yelled. "You damned kids! Come back!"

I pulled the key out of my pocket and yanked open the truck door, looking over my shoulder to check out Jasper and David. Jasper struggled to pull David into the truck. "You're too heavy! You've got to help!" Jasper shouted. Suddenly David was in, and I heard Jasper's triumphant yell as the tailgate slammed in place.

I slid into the front seat and turned the key in the ignition. The engine started instantly and I grasped the gear lever, squinting to read the letters on the dial. This truck wasn't like Gram's—which was the only thing I'd ever driven. I crossed my fingers and shoved the gear lever to "D"—and the truck door opened and a strong hand grabbed my arm.

I kicked sideways at the man with my left foot. He didn't let go. He pulled me toward the open door while I held on to the steering wheel with both hands, screaming at the top of my lungs.

He wouldn't let go! I slammed my foot down on the accelerator and the truck bucked off the driveway into the rough grass. The man's full weight hung from my arm and I was afraid he'd break it. "Let go!" I screamed. "Let go of me!"

I heard a shot.

"Don't shoot! You'll hit me!" the man yelled at his friends. He still wouldn't let go of my arm.

The truck bounced into the air and landed again, jarring me so hard that I thought I must have chipped my clenched teeth. The man scrabbled with his free hand to grab the door, missed and dropped away. I didn't let go of the wheel with my left hand to pull the door shut —I was too scared. I didn't even know if David and Jasper were still in the back of the truck. All I knew was that I had to get out of there.

I turned toward the driveway, bouncing across rough ground, and as soon as we hit the gravel, I stepped on the gas as hard as I could. Rocks splattered behind me, thrown up by the spinning tires. The truck slithered sideways and the door shut by itself as I turned out on the highway.

I looked back. No one was following from the farm, but a black four-wheel-drive truck pulled out from a clump of trees across the highway and roared after me.

Who's that? I thought, panicked. I gripped the wheel hard and looked up in the rearview mirror. The black truck was right behind, close.

I'd never driven so fast and I didn't know where I was going, either. If there'd been time, I would have burst into tears. Once again I looked in the rearview mirror, and the black truck was still there.

Something slammed against the window behind me. I twisted my head around for a second. Jasper! He was knocking on the glass. I bent over the wheel and increased speed. If Jasper hadn't fallen out, then David was probably safe, too.

But the black truck was gaining.

Ahead of me I saw a small red car poking along the highway. I was overtaking it and would either have to slow down or pass it. I was going too fast for the limited experience I'd had in passing—I was going too fast for the experience I'd had in driving, period.

I honked the truck horn and swerved out to pass the red car. At least there wasn't a car coming from the opposite direction! I eased back in place and looked in the mirror. The black truck was still behind me.

I gripped the wheel. The first time I saw a house, I was going to pull in. Someone would help us. I was going to pull in and start honking and screaming, and the people who lived there would come out and . . .

And do what? The men following me in the black truck were dangerous. They carried weapons. And they were mean. They wouldn't care if I asked someone for help, because unless that someone had a weapon too, he would be no threat to them.

Ahead of us, going up a long hill, I saw a line of cars following a tanker truck. There was no way I could pass all those cars and a big truck, too, not that close to the top of a hill. There were no side roads I could turn on. There were no houses, just miles of thick, unbroken woods.

And the black truck was still following close behind, but now there were two gray cars behind me, too.

It was hopeless. I didn't know enough about driving to figure my way out of this. I had done the very best I could and it wasn't good enough.

I let up on the gas pedal and took my place in the long line of cars following the tanker truck. I didn't know what would happen next—but the army probably wouldn't do anything to us as long as we were in this line.

The truck wobbled a little. No, I was the one wobbling. I was shaking so hard that I couldn't hold the wheel straight. Ahead of me, looking through the back window of a station wagon, a little blond girl waved and grinned. She was safe in a car with her parents, and if she was lucky, she'd never know how I felt.

The black truck and both gray cars dropped back but still followed persistently. The tanker topped the hill and I expected the line of cars to start moving faster, but it didn't. And when I got to the top, I saw why. Down the hill, two more gray cars were parked across the highway.

Roadblock.

But there were several narrow dirt roads leading away from the highway on this side of the hill. Recklessly, I skidded onto the first one.

Chapter Sixteen

IT ONLY TOOK ME seconds to realize I'd chosen the wrong road. This one, not much more than a dirt track, ended after a sharp curve not more than three hundred feet from the highway. I slammed on the brakes and narrowly missed a couple of picnic tables. The truck skidded and spun until I faced the way I'd come, but I didn't waste any time checking out who was following us or berating myself for being the world's worst driver—I leaped out of the truck and ran around to the back.

Jasper and David were on their feet, staggering toward the tailgate. Jasper's face was scarlet and his glasses hung from one ear. "You nearly killed us, Caroline!" he shouted.

"Get out and run!" I screamed as I let down the tailgate. "Run as fast as you can." And I pointed downhill, into the cool green trees.

But Jasper yelled "No!" and pointed the other way, uphill. Poor silent David nearly fell on him when he jumped off the truck, but

Jasper kept his balance, grabbed David's good arm, and started hauling him toward the woods—back up the hill.

"We're going the wrong way," I panted as I followed. I heard the growl of an engine and knew the black truck was coming—was nearly there! We ducked under trees and ran, stumbling and gasping, until the truck engine stopped. Jasper fell flat deliberately and pulled David with him. Not knowing what else to do, I crept close to them on my hands and knees.

"They'll expect us to go downhill because it's easier," Jasper whispered in my ear. "And they won't expect us to go back the way we came."

That bit of wisdom came from either Bugman or the junior rescue volunteers, I thought. Wherever Jasper learned it, I was grateful because I heard men's voices faintly behind us and they weren't getting any closer.

But I also heard more engines on the dirt track from the highway.

"Come on!" Jasper hissed, pulling David to his feet. "We have to keep going."

David's face was gray and sick and I wasn't sure he even understood what was happening. I had to keep my eyes away from the horrible infected wound on his arm while I slid my arm around his waist to help him walk.

"Sorry," he mumbled. "Caroline, I'm sorry. Just let me stay here. I don't think I can keep up with you."

"You will!" I whispered savagely. "You will too keep up."

Jasper, half running, stayed ahead of us, but he looked back every minute or so to check our progress. David was heavy but I refused to think about that—I was so scared I think I could have carried him. When we stumbled—and we did, over and over—I got him up on his feet almost instantly. Once when we fell I lost sight of Jasper and for a moment I panicked, but then Jasper came scuttling back, appearing out of a clump of bushes like a small, dirty, wild animal. "We're almost back to the highway," he whispered.

"We can't go there!" I protested.

"They won't look hard for us by the highway." Jasper bent and squirreled off, and I had no choice but to follow. He was the one who was supposed to know how to survive in the woods. I just doubted that his training included hiding out from lunatics.

I could hear the traffic sounds from the highway when Jasper finally stopped. He helped me pull David under the dark, sheltering branches of a fir, and while we squatted close to the trunk, we scraped out a hollow for David to lie in.

David groaned once while we were easing him into this makeshift bed. "You'll be all right here," I whispered. "We'll take care of you and get help. Everything is going to be all right now."

But David couldn't hear me. His eyes were half open and he breathed irregularly through his mouth. The terrible wound on his arm had broken open, leaking blood and yellowish fluid.

Jasper and I exchanged glances. "Should we go out on the highway and stop a car?" I asked.

"What if it's the wrong car?"

I leaned against the tree trunk, thinking. "You could hide alongside the highway and wait until you see a car that looks like it has a family in it," I suggested finally.

"By the time I find out that it has a family in it, it'll be gone," Jasper said. He fiddled with his glasses until they sat a little straighter on his nose, then took out his lottery tickets and shuffled them nervously while he thought. "Anyway, we're on the wrong side of that roadblock we saw. No matter who picked us up, the crazy guys will get us at the roadblock."

I gnawed one of my broken fingernails. "Somebody is going to turn them in for stopping cars like that. Sooner or later the highway patrol will be here."

Jasper considered this. "Yeah. I could wait by the highway until I see a patrol car and then jump up and wave my arms."

It sounded like a plan that might work. "Go do it," I said. "I'll stay here and take care of David. If all three of us go, there's more chance of getting caught."

Jasper looked dubiously at me. "You won't go charging around in the brush and making a lot of noise, will you? If they didn't hear us getting up here, it will be a miracle."

"If they heard us, they'd be here," I said. "I can handle it. You go wait for a patrol car."

"Okay." He thrust his lottery tickets at me. "If anything happens and you have to leave here, mark your trail in a couple of places." Then he crept out from under the branches and I didn't hear another sound. For a moment I thought he hadn't left, but when I parted the branches and looked, he was gone. Bugman really did know his way around the woods.

I strained my ears, listening to the hum of

the traffic a few hundred feet away, waiting for the screech of tires that would mean a state patrolman was making an emergency stop for Jasper. But the hum was steady, a hypnotic drone that deadened my senses. After I shoved the lottery tickets in my pocket, I stretched out on the ground next to David.

I sat up, shocked awake by the sound of gunfire. Holding my breath, I listened and waited. Another shot, then two more in quick succession.

They were coming from farther down the wooded slope, where we had abandoned the truck. But who was shooting?

And who were they shooting at?

I crawled out from under the branches, looking in the direction Jasper had taken. He was going toward the highway, not down the slope. He wouldn't have had any reason to go back in the direction of the truck.

Unless he'd been seen near the highway and took off running in any old direction, just to get away. Was it Jasper they were shooting at?

I crept back under the tree. "David," I whispered. "David." But he didn't hear me.

I didn't want to leave him but I had to find out if Jasper was still beside the highway. I crawled out from under the tree again and headed toward the hum of traffic.

The highway was farther away than I thought. I couldn't go in a straight line, either, for here and there fallen trees and mounds of brush forced me out and around, costing both time and energy and I didn't have them to spare. More than anything, I wanted to yell Jasper's name.

When I stood at the edge of the woods at last, it seemed that I had been away from David for hours. But the sun still hung in almost the same place in the bright blue sky. The problem was me—I had long since lost any ability to judge how much time was passing. How long had we been caught up in this awful mess? Days? Weeks? I rubbed dirty fists in my eyes and blinked. And where was Jasper, anyway?

I could see cars from where I stood, although I was sure no one in those cars saw me because I was sheltered in the gloom of the woods. Traffic was heavy in all lanes. I dropped down and crawled on my hands and knees through the dry brush between the woods and the highway. And I watched for a glimpse of Jasper. If he had come this way, he'd left no trace.

Then I heard the sound I wanted to hear more than any other—the sound of brakes. Cautiously, I raised my head.

Jasper was standing not ten feet from me, waving his arms. At the edge of the highway, a man climbed out of a gray car. Mike Slattery!

I leaped up. "No!" I screamed at Jasper, who was running toward Mike. "Jasper, don't! He's one of them!"

Jasper hesitated, looking back at me in surprise. That moment of hesitation was all Mike Slattery needed. He lunged for Jasper and caught him.

I ran forward, raising my fists over my head. We couldn't have gone through all this, only to be captured again. I couldn't stand any more. "Let him go!" I screamed.

Another man hopped out of the gray car, a man in a splotched uniform. I recognized him! It was the man who tried to start the engine of the camper the men were going to use to take us from the farm to the mountain cabin. I stopped in my tracks.

Two of them? Could I get Jasper away from two of them?

The man in the uniform started toward me. "Hey!" he called out to me.

I turned and ran for the woods.

Oh, Jasper, I'm sorry! I thought. I can't fight off two of them. And what's going to happen to David if we're both caught?

But I hated myself as I sprinted through the brush toward the woods. And when I finally plunged into the cool shadows, I was crying.

David hadn't moved since I left. I flopped down next to him under the spreading branches, breathing hard and pressing one hand against the stitch in my side.

I hurt in a hundred places. My arms were bleeding from cuts and scratches, and somewhere during my flight from the highway, I'd twisted my ankle. The pain was so awful that I wondered how I'd run on it.

"David," I whispered, "we're in terrible trouble."

But David didn't hear. His arm had stopped bleeding again, but angry red skin swelled around the gaping mouth of the wound. I leaned my head against his chest and sobbed.

We had to get out of here. Jasper trusted Mike and he'd tell where we were.

But wait. There was the other man, the one in the uniform. Jasper wouldn't trust him. He'd know now that Mike was one of them so he'd keep our secret.

Then David moaned my name and reached for me with his good arm. His trembling hand smoothed my tangled hair. "You have to leave me now," he whispered. "I'll be okay. You go, right now. Take care of my girl for me."

I heard Jasper's voice and the crackle of brush being broken by careless walkers. The men were coming—and Jasper was leading them straight to us.

Chapter Seventeen

I CRAWLED OUT FROM under the branches and grabbed a rock. I was ready to bash the first person I saw in the head. David and I weren't going to be captured again!

Then my common sense caught up with me. There was no way I could overwhelm grown men with a rock. Somehow we had to get away—but David was unconscious.

I'd have to get them to follow me away from David, and when I could, I'd come back for him. And since Jasper was with them, what better way to lead them away than with Jasper's own trail markers?

I pulled the lottery tickets out of my pocket and dropped one—the one that might be a winner—in clear view a few feet from the tree. And then I ran in the opposite direction from the sounds the men and Jasper were making. And I dropped two more lottery tickets. Jasper would think that David and I had left our hiding place for some reason but wanted him to follow.

In spite of my ankle, I ran through the woods, and I didn't make as much noise as I did the first time I escaped from the men. But then, I'd had quite a bit of experience in sneaking around. After a few minutes, when I couldn't hear the noise they made anymore, I started uphill, intending to circle around and approach the tree from the other direction when the time seemed right. *See, Jasper?* I thought. *I'm getting to be almost as clever as you are. You've been a good teacher.*

And that's when I fell. I tripped hard over a log I didn't see in the ferns, wrenching my sore ankle and plunging sideways to land on a half-buried slab of rock. For a moment my ankle hurt so bad I couldn't breathe.

I had to wait until I didn't see stars anymore, and then I tried to get to my knees. I fell back with a gasp that would have been a scream if I hadn't been so out of breath.

Seconds ticked by while I forced myself to wait and gather strength. Then I tried to get up again. The pain in my ankle shot up to my knee—I rolled helplessly over on my side. I needed something to use as a cane or crutch, so I scratched around in the ferns, looking for anything that would do. The dead branches I found were old and rotten. I could have pulled myself up using a tree for balance, but the nearest tree was out of reach.

I crawled then, dragging myself toward the shelter of low-hanging cedar branches. I'd rest for a while, then pull myself up and make my way from tree to tree, if necessary. Somehow

I'd find a way. I'd get out of this and get David out of it, too.

"You can stop now, Caroline."

Mike Slattery was behind me. I didn't have to look up and back to know—I recognized that cool voice. My hand closed around a rock and I rolled over and threw it as hard as I could.

Mike dodged the rock easily—it landed at Jasper's feet.

"Caroline!" he yelled furiously. "You nearly hit me! Quit that and let us rescue you!"

I burst into tears and snatched up another rock, holding it ready. "You let me alone!" I screamed. Rescue? Who was Jasper kidding? He may have thought Mike was rescuing us but I knew better.

Mike reached one hand into a pocket. He's going to shoot me now, I thought. Somewhere far away I heard the wail of an ambulance—or maybe the police—but the sound was too far away to mean help for me. I dropped the rock just as Mike pulled his hand back out of his pocket.

He held a small, neat leather folder open so that I could see inside. I stared at it without comprehension.

"Mike's a federal marshal!" Jasper howled. "I told you he was okay."

I shook my head stubbornly. "I saw that man at the house give him a signal. They knew each other, Jasper."

"He's a marshal, too," Mike said. He slid the leather folder back into his pocket and unhooked a small radio from his belt. "You can straighten it all out later. First, let's get Caroline out of here." He muttered into the radio, giving someone directions, and I rolled over on my stomach and buried my face in my hands. I couldn't believe him because it seemed to me that I had been running and hiding my whole life and maybe that's all there was to life—running and hiding.

"Will you help David this time?" I asked finally, not really expecting anything.

"David's on his way to the hospital," Mike said when he fastened the radio back to his belt. "That's where you're going now."

"We followed the lottery tickets to find you," Jasper said. "I taught you that, Caroline, except that you should have saved the good one until last. What if we hadn't found it?"

I ignored Jasper. "How did you know where we were?" I asked Mike.

"We knew where you were from the time I stopped by that farm with David's horse. You say you saw someone give me a signal? He worked undercover with the survivalists for months. After he let me know they had you, we simply followed you from one place to another, waiting for a time when we could get you away safely. That young woman back at the farm created a new problem when she gave you the truck key. Fortunately the undercover man saw her disabling the cars so the survivalists couldn't follow you. She admitted it, told him about the key, and we had cars waiting to help you."

"Yeah, and then you ruined everything," Jasper interrupted. "Maybe I didn't know marshals were trying to help us, but I knew you turned the wrong way. I knocked on the window but you kept right on going."

"What wrong way!" I cried. "What are you talking about?"

"We expected you to turn west, toward home," Mike said. "You fooled us when you turned east. And the survivalists in the truck were right behind you. If you'd turned west, we had cars to cut them off. It took time to set up something else."

"The roadblock," I said.

"And you surprised us by turning off the highway," Mike said. "We tried to get you out of the line of fire and you kept getting back into it."

"Next time I'll try to do better." I smiled at him weakly.

He patted my shoulder and grinned down at me. "You did fine, Caroline. You got Jasper and David away from the survivalists. Your parents are going to be proud of you."

Several men trotted up then and they unrolled a stretcher for me. I concentrated on being brave and not crying when my leg was moved, but I wasn't concentrating so hard that I missed Jasper being Jasper again.

"Hey, Mike," he said, "Can you use your radio to talk to someone on the telephone?"

"It can be arranged. Why?"

Jasper rubbed his nose and knocked his glasses crooked. "I need to talk to Gram and find out if she let my tarantula out of the jar."

I saw Mike's mouth twitch. "Well, I might have trouble arranging a phone patch for something like that. How about calling your grandmother from the hospital? I suppose the tarantula can wait another twenty minutes."

"I don't know," Jasper said dubiously. "They get awful depressed if they're shut up very long."

A depressed tarantula. We just got out of the worst trouble we were ever in, and my cousin Jasper is worrying about the mental health of his tarantula. Some things never change. The men lifted the stretcher and filed downhill toward the highway, and Jasper stumbled alongside.

"Bugman's specially trained tarantula got shut up once . . ." he began.

"I don't want to hear about Bugman," I told him fretfully. "And I especially don't want to hear one more word about that awful spider of yours."

"Well, thanks a lot, Caroline Cartright!" Jasper squalled. "And all I did was only save your life, I hope you know. And after you nearly killed us in the truck. You are the worst driver in the whole world and maybe the whole universe."

"Jasper, if you don't shut up, I'll never go anywhere with you again," I cried.

"Hey, Jasper, you still got those cocoons?" Mike interrupted smoothly in that cool, sly way of his. "Let's have a look."

Believe it or not, Jasper still had the wretched things in a paper sack in his pocket. He pulled it out and dropped back to walk with Mike.

"Is that kid your brother?" the man carrying the head of the stretcher asked.

"No," I said tearfully. "He's nobody's brother. It's bad enough having him for a cousin. Sometimes he makes me so mad I wish I'd left him back at that farm."

The men carrying me laughed. "I don't think the survivalists want him either," one of them said. "They've got enough trouble."

Chapter Eighteen

THE DANCE WASN'T LIKE the one I dreamed about that night when we were held captive at the farm. It wasn't my prom—it was the Christmas dance at North County High. And none of the paramilitary men came in to find us and take us away again. But halfway through the wonderful evening I thought about them.

"What's wrong?" David asked, looking down at me with concern. "You shivered. Are you cold?"

The auditorium at David's high school was warm that winter evening. Too warm, actually. But still, I shivered.

David tightened his arms around me while we danced. "What are you thinking about? You look worried."

I laughed a little, just to prove I wasn't worried about anything. And I told him about my dream. "Tonight reminds me of the dream. I guess, for a minute, I expected those men to come in looking for us."

"They're all in jail," David reminded me. "Including Cissy's rotten husband."

"But when I had the dream," I said, "going to a dance with you seemed like the last thing in the world that could really happen. I wasn't sure we were ever going anywhere again."

David bent his head and kissed me lightly. "But here we are. Now get the dream off your mind and put me there. I've got an important question to ask you."

I leaned my head against his shoulder, glad that the band was playing a whole set of slow dances. I liked having David's arms around me. I liked it too much, probably. "Ask your question," I said. "You're catching me in a good mood tonight."

"Umm," David murmured in my ear. "I love catching you in a good mood and I want to do a lot more of it. Do you suppose your folks would let you stay with your grandmother when school gets out in June?"

I grinned to myself. I had anticipated this and had already persuaded my parents to let me spend most of the summer with Gram. They weren't hard to convince—they had to make a lot of short business trips during the warm months, and after the events of last summer always wanted to know where I was. And even after last summer's ordeal, Granite Ridge was safer and more peaceful than Seattle.

"I think my folks would let me stay in Granite Ridge this summer," I told David. "In fact, I'm sure of it."

"But do you want to?"

I slipped my arms around his neck. "Oh yes!" I whispered.

When the music stopped, he led me toward the long table where my parents sat with Gram and a couple dozen other adults. The dances in Granite Ridge are usually community affairs—small towns don't waste opportunities for celebration. And since it was also Gram's birthday, my folks drove up from Seattle with Aunt Sybil and Uncle Ray—and the widely known Jasper, who was wearing the purple and gold Bugman Wonder Watch Cissy gave him before Mike Slattery and the government secret witness program helped her change her name and disappear.

I tried to ignore my cousin, choosing an empty seat as far away from him as possible. He was relatively clean that evening, but his shirt pocket was hanging from a thread and the lenses of his glasses were held in place with what looked like bits of duct tape. He didn't notice that I was ignoring him because he was listening to his very expensive personal radio through his very expensive earphones. Jasper's one good lottery ticket not only won him the tarantula (still alive and living in a box) last summer, but also five hundred dollars.

David and I exchanged smiles and we were about to tell my parents and Gram about my summer plans when Jasper leaned forward, removed the green gum from his mouth (clearing the decks for action, as it were), and yelled, "Hey, Caroline!"

Everyone winced and Aunt Sybil lifted one of Jasper's earpieces and said, "Don't yell, dear."

"Hey, Caroline!" Jasper yelled—same volume, even with his ears unplugged.

"What?" I asked. Dim warning bells were signaling me from somewhere in my subconscious.

"Guess what?" Jasper bellowed over the sounds of the band, the dancers, a hundred kids and fifty adults, and the squawking noises coming from his headphones.

"I give up," I said. "Just tell me straight."

"Oh, dear," Aunt Sybil moaned. Uncle Ray dug through his pockets, smiling glassily at me. He was looking for combat pay! I just knew it!

"I get to spend the summer at Gram's with you!" Jasper squalled. "Ain't that great?"

David's hand found mine and squeezed it. "Now I know why you were thinking about that dream," he whispered in my ear.

"I know, too," I said. "It was a premonition. He's almost as bad as the Major and his crazy army."

"It's my turn to rescue us, Caroline," David whispered. "Will you trust me?"

I leaned against him. Trust him? I wanted to believe that he could rescue us from my cousin, but I wasn't sure anyone was that crafty. "Let me put it this way," I told David. "I'm willing to have another adventure. But this time I'm not going anywhere near the ridge."

"Right. We'll stay as far away as we can get," David said.

Jasper wormed his way between us, elbowing me sharply in the ribs in his effort to get David's full attention. "Hey, David, guess what I saw in the woods down by the river? An abandoned car! I saw it this afternoon, but I didn't have time to check it out. Do you want to look it over with me tonight?"

David stood up quickly and I could see him struggling to keep from laughing. "I can't, Jasper," he said. "Right now I've got some important dancing to do." He held out his arms to me and I walked into them.

Behind me I could hear Jasper say, indignantly "Caroline! Hey, I was talking, you guys!"

David danced me clear to the other side of the auditorium and out the door. Arms around each other, we danced down the walk. I watched the cold stars spin over us, and when at last we couldn't hear the music anymore, we stopped.

"We're going to have a great summer," David whispered.

"I know," I whispered back. "Hey, David, why do you suppose anyone would abandon a car in the woods down by the river?"

"You're as bad as he is," David said, laughing.

"Jasper?" I asked incredulously. "Are you comparing me to Jasper?"

"Bright, funny, and curious. Who does that sound like?" David demanded.

"Trouble with knobs on," I told him, and

then I started laughing, too. "David," I said, "did I ever tell you how much I miss you when I'm not here and you're not in Seattle?"

He kissed the tip of my nose. "You've mentioned it but I'd like to hear it again."

JEAN THESMAN lives near Seattle with her family and several dogs.